Massacre
at the
Comic Shop

Other books by Nick Ulanowski:

As the Moonlight Shines

Diesel Doctrine and the Temporarily Embarrassed Millionaires

American Bug

Massacre at the Comic Shop

Nick Ulanowski

Massacre at the Comic Shop

ISBN:
Paperback: 979-8-9883838-0-2
E-Book: 979-8-9883838-1-9

Printed in the United States or United Kingdom by Lightning Source.

Written by Nick Ulanowski
Edited by Dierdre Roberts
Front & back cover art by Kevin P. West
Logo & cover design by Audrey Clément
Interior design by B. Clay Moore

10 9 8 7 6 5 4 3 2 1

To my friend who, during the weekend of a comic
book convention, heard me waking up screaming
in our hotel room:
Sorry about that.

FOREWORD

A comic shop can be a scary place.

Not generally in the traditional bats and spiders kind of way – though there are lots of those.

And not generally in the existential terror kind of way - unless you ponder how many hours an assortment of sweaty cartoonists must have slaved over their many art boards to yield this shopful of parchment plastered with cartoons.

And not even really in the slasher movie sort of way - as a knife wielding maniac lurking behind the leaden box of unsold '90s comics is probably out of shape, softened by years of RPGs and non-diet Mountain Dews, and easily left, wheezing at the register.

No, the way they can be scary is in the strange tribalism they can house. They've become rife in recent years with a certain kind of "fan," one who, at best believes the newcomer reader to be beneath them, an unwelcome interloper, at worst, who seethes with a barely contained animosity at women, people of color, and gays for daring to intrude into HIS fantasy world and asking to see themselves represented. Ask any comic curious woman or non-white male or not-straight person if they've ever felt the searing gaze of some Gatekeeper of Geekery, and you'll nearly universally get the same answer.

It is at the corners of this reality that Nick Ulanowki's MASSACRE AT THE COMIC SHOP steps, a rollicking, bloody metaphor for an invisible violence. It's a satire of the horrors that lurk in the imaginations of the bereaved, hardcore fanboy, playing out beside romantic pairings of androids and aliens, alongside team-ups of intercorporate, intellectual properties. It's a world Nick knows well, and one he hopes... no, demands be better.

And so, with this in mind, enjoy the terrors imagined on the page – perhaps as a cathartic relief for the real menaces experienced on the way to purchase this book.

Tim Seeley
Chicago, Illinois
February 5th, 2023

Tim Seeley has drawn several different comic book series including G.I JOE, HALLOWEEN, WILDCATS and EXSANGUINE. His writing work includes New York Times bestselling HACK/SLASH, NIGHTWING, BATMAN ETERNAL and the critically acclaimed REVIVAL.

Prologue
The Grind

The sky is pitch black. If there are any stars in the sky, they must be invisible due to the city's light pollution.

I look up and I take a deep breath, thinking about all the bullshit I deal with at this job.

Off in the distance, I see the remnants of abandoned industry. But here, where I stand, I hear the pounding sounds of dozens of trucks. They're filled with over-the-road truck drivers who are transporting goods across the United States.

Perhaps the sound I hear is more of a loud hum than a pounding sensation. It's the sound of idling engines. And it's a constant stream of aggressive, whooshing noises that trucks make whenever drivers hit the brakes. After many nights of normalizing and drowning out these sounds, the time I spend in the lot has become oddly relaxing. I sometimes end up thinking about the big picture and the direction of my life here more than anywhere else.

I'm outside of the truck stop gathering all the garbage bags next to each diesel pump. It'll be several hours before my shift ends. Because it's later in the evening, not many customers are buying showers anymore. I no longer have to constantly clean the shower rooms and prepare clean towels to maintain their availability. I can finally get this other task done that's expected of me every day.

"Fuck this shit," I murmur as the side of the plastic bag breaks open, spilling wet garbage all over the ground. Fortunately, I have protective gloves and a whole roll of garbage bags. I can turn this bag of garbage into two bags before carrying them to the nearby dumpster. Unlike the other truck stop where I used to work, the dumpster here has a trash compactor. It's big enough for the largest bag of garbage. Hell, it's big enough for a dozen large bags filled with garbage.

The parking lot here is much bigger than the other truck stop, the one where I used to work with Holt, Calvin, Melissa and Brad. And despite what certain reviewers may claim on Facebook and Yelp, there are no lot lizards roaming around. Instead, there are local police officers standing guard everywhere. Although quite frankly, I think I'd prefer the former. The worst thing a hooker will ever do is harass you. A cop just might kill you.

My name is Mitchell Derrick, and I've been working for this company for way too fucking long.

The old truck stop didn't have a trash compactor. However, a bigger truck stop means more garbage, making this addition necessary. We also have two porters working at the same time instead of only one. We have a downstairs porter who mostly cleans the bathrooms and floors and an upstairs porter who mostly cleans and maintains the showers. I'm the upstairs porter, but I also clean and maintain the lots outside. I like working alongside another porter better, but the job is still a lot of the same old bullshit.

At the old truck stop, Cindy, the General Manager, posted everyone's weekly work schedule in the room where porters fold towels. She posted another copy of the schedule behind the fuel desk. When writing one week's schedule, she made a last-minute change. But instead of replacing the copies of the schedule in both rooms, she only replaced the one in the porter's room. So, in the porter's room, it said I was working but the copy behind the fuel desk said I was off for the day. When I called Petrol to ask if I had to work tomorrow, Melissa looked at the copy posted behind the fuel desk and told me I didn't.

As a result, I didn't show up to work that day because I didn't realize I was supposed to. I'd never been a "no call, no show" before, as Craig, the former General Manager, could tell you. Brad, the shift lead, outright said that it was 100% Cindy's fault for not updating the schedule in both locations. He described it as being "messed up" if Cindy were to fire me. But this was the same GM who fired a cashier on the first day she transferred there. And she was already mad about the several times I was about ten minutes late.

Before I could get fired, I texted Craig. I told him that I'd take him up on that offer of transferring to the truck stop where he transferred to. And that's how I started working at the new location where I am today.

Politicians and the media keep saying that America's Great Recession is coming to an end. I can't tell. It's still the same old shit for me. I can't believe I've been working for this company for nearly four years and I'm still a porter. I'm still at the very bottom of the totem pole. I've had no advancement or even a raise.

When I transferred to this new truck stop with Craig, I was hopeful for a new beginning. I no longer feel like I've gotten one. But at least I was able to write a short story titled *Back on the Grind*. It's loosely based on my experiences at my former truck stop workplace.

After I bounced off ideas for the story with Holt, I posted it in a blog. A publisher eventually picked it up for a short story anthology. I couldn't be prouder of this accomplishment. *Back on the Grind* was about people I used to know at the old workplace. It was distinct enough from the truck stop where I currently work that my bosses never said anything about it. But then again, maybe they didn't even realize that *Back on the Grind* existed.

As I carry the garbage bags to the dumpster, I see a man in a ski mask approach me. There's a noticeable burn on the mask. I'm guessing where the back end of his jaw probably is. The man also has a black T-shirt with a drawing of a happy puppy, standing up with his back legs and begging for food.

The masked man is carrying a black lighter that he holds up to the right side of his head. He flicks the lighter repeatedly. After every few flicks, the lighter lights up. But after most flicks, the lighter just makes a snapping sound and doesn't exhaust a flame.

Click-click-snap.

Click-click-snap.

I work at a truck stop. This isn't the first time I've noticed a weirdo. So, I just go about my business, pretending like I don't notice him.

I toss the garbage bags into the dumpster. I'm about to press the button to start the trash compactor when the man starts running towards me.

I jolt around and say, "Woah there, buddy. What's up?" I extend my palms out as if to say "stop."

The man in the ski mask socks me in the jaw. I fall back into the metal dumpster. Reflexively, I reduce the weight of the impact with my elbows. Because the trash compacter's height is less than mine, I don't hit my head, but the pain is still intense. I feel it on my face, elbows, back and even my legs.

Before I can recover, he pulls out a knife and stabs me repeatedly in the stomach. I fall to the ground. The pain has now graduated from intense to excruciating.

"I read your short story, *Back on the Grind*. It was good. I enjoyed it," he says.

The man lifts me up and throws me into the trash compactor. He presses the Start button. My body sinks deeper and deeper into the bags of garbage. I try to stand up so I can jump and climb out. But then I feel it. My feet. My shoes. They're completely crushed.

"You won't have to work at a fucking truck stop anymore, Mitch," the man in the mask says.

I scream out for help. No one comes.

With my feet turned to mush, I fall over and hit my head on the metal side of the trash compactor. I feel the blood drip down my forehead as my body sinks deeper and deeper, slowly crushing me to death.

Chapter 1

Nine years later…

"Superman is the first superhero ever created. He's a refugee from the planet Krypton. He was created by two Jewish men in the 1930s during the height of global anti-Semitism.' You can't divorce the comic book medium from politics. That's about as ridiculous as 'apolitical' punk rock."

It was just another Wednesday at Galaxy's Comics & Games – the most popular day of the week for regular customers to pick up their comic book subscriptions.

David was standing near the cash register and in the middle of another one of his rants. His quieter friend Foggy was standing in front of the counter nearby, flipping through one of the shop's binders of Magic: The Gathering cards for sale.

"First superhero? What about those pulp magazine characters from the 1920s and '30s like the Shadow?" I replied.

"No one gives a fuck about the Shadow! What I'm saying is –"

"No one cares about the Shadow?" I interrupted. "But he's the Shadow! How can you not care about him? Are you saying nobody cares about Poochie from *The Simpsons*? Are you saying Groot is not the most important character in the MCU?"

David laughed and said, "God dammit, Eric. You know what I fucking mean. *Action Comics #1* is widely considered to be the first superhero comic. And my point is this ComicsGate guy on Twitter didn't know what the hell he was talking about."

"Yeah, they usually don't," I replied.

David is one of the regulars at the comic shop I own. He's also one of my best friends. Every Monday night when the shop is closed, we hang out and watch movies and shows – sometimes at my house and sometimes at his. He's also at the shop almost every Wednesday, picking up the comic books in his pull list and hanging out.

A pull list is a subscription service available at every local comic shop. Customers set up "pull lists" when they don't want to miss an issue of a comic book. Shops special order these books for subscribing customers in addition to the inventory that's put on the shelf. This means a customer's responsibility is to come to the shop and pick up their subscriptions at least once a month. Many shops will drop you if you fail to meet this minimum requirement.

I've allowed customers to keep their books in their pull list box for months on end. David says I'm too nice and shouldn't do this. But then again, David has waited weeks before to pay for books in his box even after he was raving about how much he was looking forward to it. But unlike these other customers, it's never for more than just a few weeks – certainly not months on end.

While David is in massive student loan debt, he still makes relatively good money. He's an attorney who works at a legal aid organization. Nonetheless, David says sometimes his funds are already allocated so he can't pick up his books this week. However, he still consistently buys all his subscriptions at least once a month.

David and I are both on the autism spectrum. At the same time, let's face it, there's no shortage of neurodivergent people inside the walls of the comic shop, especially compared to the world outside. There are folks here who can rattle off lists of titles and names like an encyclopedia but can't remember what we had for lunch yesterday.

"It just makes me so mad though. These clowns feel so entitled to these characters, but they don't even understand them. And it's hard for me to ignore it when they're harassing artists I love online," David said.

"Yeah, I get it. I just don't get involved. It's too much," I said.

"I agree," Foggy said. "Don't feed the trolls, David." Over the years, I've started to feel close to Foggy. But I suppose you could say my friendship with Foggy was mostly by way of David. I considered him a friend, sure, but he was still more so a friend of a friend.

Foggy comes to the shop almost every Wednesday with David. He flips through the binders of Magic: The Gathering cards for sale while David chats with me and others. Foggy is always on the hunt for a good Magic card to add to his decks and his collection. He's sometimes here on Friday nights for the Magic tournaments as well, but he mostly plays at friends' houses.

I'm in my early thirties. Both David and Foggy are white guys in their mid-thirties with brown hair, beards and glasses. While David insists that he's a redhead, he really isn't. I guess he was more redheaded when he was younger, but his hair is mostly just brown today.

According to David, many people who know Foggy outside of the Galaxy's Comics & Games see him as a louder, more belligerent guy. In other words, he's more like David. However, that's not generally how I know Foggy to be. I have heard him riled up before at Friday Night Magic. However, he's usually pretty quiet, especially when he comes to the shop with David on Wednesdays.

Foggy has a speech impediment, but I've never noticed it at the shop. David and Foggy have told me that his invisible disability impacted him more as a kid. I've been told that in middle school, where they first became friends, David would sometimes finish Foggy's sentences for him. He did this when Foggy was stuttering and having trouble getting the words out of his mouth. Foggy said this was helpful and he viewed it as David sticking up for him.

"I don't even use Twitter anymore. I got so sick of those hashtag 'gate' people in everyone's replies. Why spend my time reading that when I could be looking at pictures of cats and blu-rays on Instagram?" Foggy said.

"Well, I wouldn't say that. I just don't want to think about it, okay? I don't engage with them," I said

"Yeah, well, someone needs to put these whiny-ass, right-wing man-babies in their fucking place," David said.

Foggy smirked and replied, "Sure, you're all big and bad until your phone is blowing up every few seconds. We were supposed to be watching *Diary of the Dead*. But instead of watching the movie, you were staring at your phone and freaking out because some asshole with a hundred thousand followers quote tweeted you."

"Man, fuck off. It's not like we hadn't seen *Diary of the Dead* before – the best zombie movie ever made," David said, laughing.

"I think you mean *Dawn of the Dead*," Foggy replied, teasing him.

"Yeah, but David," I interjected. "Don't you usually run a block bot when that happens?" referring to a Google Chrome extension app that allows Twitter users to block every single person who follows someone who is bothering them.

"Yeah, motherfucker, you got like a hundred bazillion people on your block list," Foggy said loudly.

"Okay, fine. It's too much for me too sometimes!" David admitted. "But I took the heat off a woman in the comic book industry who I'm a fan of. Those assholes would've been harassing her if I hadn't temporarily directed their attention to me. So, I still see it as time well spent."

Chapter 2

Before I was the sole owner, Galaxy's Comics & Games was co-owned by my cousin Jeremy and me. We bought the shop from its previous owner, Luke, or "L.P." as everyone called him, who wanted to retire.

Under L.P.'s ownership, the shop's name was The Galaxy. The comic book selection was more limited than it is today. There were only comic book issues and no trade paperbacks or hardcovers. There wasn't as wide of a selection of gaming supplies either, especially for games other than Magic: The Gathering and Dungeons & Dragons. So, when we bought The Galaxy, Jeremy and I rebranded it with a new and slightly different name – Galaxy's Comics & Games. However, some regular customers, especially longtime ones, still affectionally call the store "the Galaxy."

When Jeremy co-owned Galaxy's Comics & Games, he still had his office job that he'd be at most of the week. However, Galaxy's has been my entire livelihood since day one. I quit my job as a page at the library to run this comic shop.

After a few years had passed, Jeremy got engaged and moved further away to live with his fiancé. He sold his share of the shop, his half, to me. Now, without Jeremy's help, I work six days a week. My father is the accountant for Galaxy's, and my mother will occasionally run the cash register when I'm unavailable. However, I'm the only owner of the shop now.

I still love comic books. As a comic shop owner, I'd probably be miserable if I didn't. But at the same time, since I'm constantly surrounded by them, I'm less enthused about comic books than I used to be. When I have downtime at work, I usually watch YouTube, listen to podcasts and scroll Discord and Twitter. I'll occasionally read a new comic that interests me but certainly not every day. And when I get home from work, I've already had enough of comics. Comics are my job, so reading them at home is generally not something that's appealing like it once was.

Also, if I'm being honest, toxic fans online have reduced my enthusiasm for comic books. I understand that it's just a small minority of comic book fans who are very vocal. However, this doesn't really make me feel better.

Whenever someone who isn't a regular customer walks into Galaxy's Comics & Games, I can't help but wonder: are they a part of the right-wing, online harassment campaign? Are they someone who complains about so-called "SJWs" and "forced diversity" ruining comic books? Is this person a part of the online mob who harassed a Marvel Comics writer until she deleted her Twitter? Is this stranger who walks into Galaxy's Comics & Games the same person who anonymously told me to kill myself because I liked *Star Wars: The Last Jedi*?

My social anxiety doesn't help. If someone is a regular customer or a friend, I'll usually make conversation. But if someone is a stranger, I'm much less likely to talk. While I want Galaxy's to be a welcoming environment, I have my limitations.

It was early in the evening. Me and David continued to chat while Foggy flipped through a binder of Magic cards. As we chatted, two customers walked into the store. It was a man and a woman who looked like they were in their early twenties. They had their arms around each other.

"Hello, welcome to Galaxy's Comics and Games," I said.

"Whattup? We walked here from the Asian fusion restaurant down the street. We've never been in a comic shop before," the man said.

David's face lit up after he said this. He firmly believes that comics are for everyone. "Comics are a medium, not a genre" is one of his favorite things to say. David believes in the power of this storytelling medium, and he wants everyone to experience it. Galaxy's Comics & Games is like his church. Comic books are scripture. And he is the proselytizer.

After walking in the door, the customers took their arms and hands off one another. They began walking back and forth, looking at the wall of new comic books.

"Josh, they have quite a variety of different *Power Rangers* comics. I didn't even know there were *Power Rangers* comics," the woman said.

David walked up to two of them and said, "Are you guys looking for anything in particular?"
The man replied, "No, me and my Tinder date, Dezi here, are just browsing."

Josh grabbed a comic book off the wall and showed it to Dezi.

"What the hell? Look at this," he said.

His face twisted into an expression of disgust. Perhaps he was exaggerating for comedic effect to impress his date, but the feeling of revulsion seemed genuine.

Josh showed the comic book to David and said, "Bro, some-one sliced this guy's hand off. That's brutal! I didn't know they were allowed to put something like this on the cover."

David laughed and replied, "Yeah, *Grimm Tales of Terror* is a great, horror comic. It's kind of like *Tales from the Crypt* but updated for modern times. Pretty much every issue ends with someone getting what's coming to them. Also, *Grimm Tales of Terror* is like a love letter to urban legends and the public domain. Every issue is self-contained. That one is a modern retelling of *The Monkey's Paw*."

"The Monkey's… what?" Deiz said, giggling. David's smile turned to a frown.

Without skipping a beat, David perked up again and said, "There's something for everyone in the comic shop! If you guys aren't horror fans, I'd be happy to recommend something else. Just let me know! I'll be right over there talking to Eric."

David pointed to me. I was standing a few feet away from them.

"Thanks, bro," the man said. "So, how you like working at a comic shop?"

"Oh, I don't work here," David replied. "I just love recommending comics to people."

Foggy let out a quiet chuckle as he continued to flip through the binder of Magic: The Gathering cards nearby. Even though he was listening, I'm assuming these two customers were paying no attention to him.

These weren't the first non-regular customers to come in here on a Wednesday night and mistake David for an employee. Although this was presumably because of his behavior, not his dress attire. Unlike me, David wasn't wearing a red T-shirt with a drawing of the planet Saturn and the Galaxy's Comics & Games logo. He was wearing a black Star Wars T-shirt that said "rebellious."

I chimed in and said, "Yeah, this is my shop. But I don't always feel comfortable recommending books. So, it works out that my friend David likes to recommend them."

"Oh, okay," Josh said.

It's true. Unlike David, I don't really feel confident making recommendations unless I'm talking to a friend. On numerous occasions, David has convinced a customer to buy a book that I wouldn't have even thought to say anything about.

But on the flip side, David will sometimes suggest to me that an upcoming comic book series or run will be the hot, new thing. Because of his recommendations, I'll order a bunch of copies for the shop. But when the time comes, it isn't the hot, new thing after all. Unsold copies collect dust on the walls. And unsold comic books can't be returned to the distributors, Diamond or Lunar.

When this happens, it's not David's fault per se. I still made the choice to stock the book with as many copies as I did. And to be clear, his predictions can be right too. Sometimes, when his predictions are wrong and I ordered too many copies of the book, David will buy every remaining copy. He'll list them for sale in his eBay store and either make a very small profit or break even. But like anyone else, David only has so much time and money. He's already spending a lot of it at Galaxy's for his own reading and his own collection. Often, I end up having to stuff these unsold comic books into the back issue bins near the back of the store.

At the end of the day, I still appreciated David's suggestions for the shop. Because I'm mostly just a fan of superhero comics, but he's very passionate about all kinds of other comics as well. I want to be able to stock a variety of books in the store. And David can be quite helpful in this regard.

"Woah, holy shit, what the hell is this?" Josh said before grabbing the latest issue of *Vampirella* off the shelf. His eyes widened. He showed it to his companion.

"She's a big-tittied, goth girlfriend," Dezi said.
David was starting to look uncomfortable, but he continued to talk to them.

"That's another excellent, horror comic. Vampirella's costume was designed by Trina Robbins, a sex-positive feminist in the 1970s. The new writer, Christopher Priest, has really breathed new life into the character."

"That's cool, bro," Josh said. "So does she, like, suck blood and shit?"

"Chris Hemsworth is hot," Dezi interrupted before David could answer. "You guys got any *Thor* comics?" she asked.
Josh's goofy smile turned to a frown. He turned his head and stared at her.

"What?" Dezi said, giggling again.

"Yeah, we do. You're looking at the indie books right now, but I'll show you where Marvel is," David said.
Josh put the *Vampirella* comic book back on the shelf. David walked the two customers to the part of the wall that had the latest issues published by Marvel.

"Honestly, I haven't been keeping up with *Thor* since Jane Foster stopped wielding the hammer. But let me know if you guys have any more questions," David said.

"Thanks, bro," Josh said.

Chapter 3

Later in the evening, after David and Foggy left the shop, Anna stopped by to drop off and donate a new bundle of her stickers. This was at about 7:00 PM, an hour before closing time.

"Hi, welcome to Galaxy's Comics and Games," I said after the door opened. "Oh, hi, Anna!" I then said after seeing who it was.

Anna is naturally a blonde, but she dyes her hair every few months or so. This month, her bangs and the rest of her hair were bright green.

Like David, Foggy and some of the other regular customers, I considered Anna a friend. She always seemed happy not just to buy comic books but to see me.

"What's up, Eric?" Anna said.
Anna was carrying a Free Comic Book Day shopping bag, like the ones I used to give out to customers before running out of them. Anna set the bag on the counter.

"I got some new stickers for ya," Anna declared.

"Awesome!" I said. "Whatch ya got this time?"

"Some more Pikachu and some She-Hulk. I never drew She-Hulk before, but some people have been diggin' the Disney Plus show. So, why not?" she said.

"Yeah, I've been watching it with David on my days off. It's good," I said.

"I haven't seen it. I'm not really a fan of the character to be honest. She was fun to draw though!" Anna said.

"I bet," I replied.

Anna is in her mid-twenties. Ever since she was a kid, she's loved to draw. These days, she mostly draws portraits of superheroes and anime characters. In addition to selling prints and original artwork on Etsy, Anna mass produces small stickers with her drawings of superheroes and anime characters. These stickers have a white border and her Etsy store logo in the lower right-hand corner.

As is our arrangement, I throw one of Anna's stickers in customers' bags whenever they buy something. This gets the word out about Anna's artwork and Etsy store.

I enjoy being able to help promote a local artist and hopefully make Anna feel like her creativity is valid and appreciated. Even if she's never been published before, I love Anna's work. It's very eye popping and proficient. Some of her artwork is drawn right here in the shop. She occasionally sits at the gaming tables in the back of the store and scribbles in her sketchbook, especially on Friday and Saturday nights.

Anna has been a customer here for as long as I've owned the store. Unlike David and Foggy who are here just about every week, Anna tends to only be here once or twice a month. Anna has a small pull list of mostly horror comic books, and she occasionally buys manga as well. She used to subscribe to a lot of Marvel books, but she slowly unsubscribed in favor of more indie books from Dark Horse, Dynamite and Image Comics. She told me that while she still draws the characters and watches the new Marvel and DC movies, she's getting tired of superhero comics. That said, Anna never seems to get tired of *Buffy the*

Vampire Slayer comics. For as long as I've known her, she's read every single Buffy universe (or "Buffyverse") comic book.

On the walls of Galaxy's Comics & Games, there are four different original pieces I bought from Anna – portraits of Goku, the Wolf Man, Spider-Man and a drawing of Batman and Superman about to clash with one another in battle. Additionally, there are posters with images of superheroes and Magic: The Gathering characters. This includes a Marvel cover by Alex Ross and a Superman poster that showed the first 1,000 *Action Comics* covers published by DC Comics.

"Is there anything in my box?" Anna asked, referring to her pull list subscriptions.

"I don't think so, but I'll check."

"Thanks, Eric," Anna said.

"No probs," I said.

I turned around and looked through the alphabetized names. They're in big letters on pieces of cardboard dividing the comic books in everyone's subscriptions. I found Anna's pull list.

There was nothing new for her today.

In the comic book industry, comic books must be pre-ordered two months in advance from either Diamond Distribution or Lunar. At Galaxy's Comics & Games, every customer's pull list is in a box with their name on it. Or more accurately, it rests in between cardboard dividers with customers' names on them. The day before the official release date, I go through all the books and put them in both pull list boxes and on the wall for other customers to purchase.

"Nope," I answered her.

"Oh, okay," Anna said.

I picked up the bag and looked through the stickers in it. There were three Pikachu and three She-Hulks.

There's a cardboard display box by the register that I use for some of the latest issues of a hot item. Right now, Galaxy's had a stack of the *Harley Quinn 25th Anniversary Special* comic books displayed upright.

I laid out the stickers next to this display. The stickers were easily visible to any customer checking out. However, they were still close enough to me so I could grab one and put it in a customer's bag.

As I was doing this, another regular customer, Blake, walked up to Anna. He had arrived here shortly after David and Foggy left. He'd been playing the Yu-Gi-Oh card game with his friends at the gaming tables in the back of the store.

Blake is in his late 20s. He's been collecting comic books, reading Manga and playing Yu-Gi-Oh since he was a teenager. He's been a regular at this shop since the previous owners ran it. I've been told he first started coming to Galaxy's when he was in high school.

These days, Blake is at Galaxy's about three times a week hanging out, socializing and playing Yu-Gi-Oh with his buddies. He's here every Friday and/or Saturday and once or twice a week in addition to that. He doesn't have a pull list but regularly buys comic books, especially superhero comics. He doesn't play Magic: The Gathering but he's still often here during Friday Night Magic. He chats with everyone, and he plays Yu-Gi-Oh with his buddies before and after the tournament.

I'm not sure, but I think sometime during Friday Night Magic is where Blake first met Anna. Anna didn't participate in the tournaments either. She'd bring her sketchbook, sit at the gaming tables and draw. I often noticed her socializing with the gamers. But a lot of the time, she kept to herself. She liked the vibes of the comic shop and the Magic tournament better than staying home and making artwork.

Blake is someone whose outgoing personality really shines. When he walks into the room, he can light it up. To Blake, the comic shop is like his bar. It's where he comes and socializes. Everyone knows his name here and he loves it. I consider him a friend – and so do a lot of people at the comic shop. I've been told he's well liked at the restaurant where he works the morning shift, too.

While I've seen Blake at David's birthday parties, I can't say I've seen him a whole lot outside of Galaxy's Comics & Games. But whenever I see him, he's always wearing an assortment of different rings and a Black Lives Matter bracelet. I think it's safe to say he's an outspoken guy. While he's less likely than David to bring it up, Blake isn't afraid to talk about politics or current events in the store. That said, he's probably a little quieter about his opinions than David. He's certainly less likely to loudly bring them up in awkward situations. Blake doesn't want to alienate people while David generally doesn't seem to care a whole lot if he does.

"Hey, Anna. How's it going? You don't have your sketchbook with you today?" Blake asked.

"No, not today. I was just dropping off some new stickers, but I can chat," Anna said.

"Yep! Pikachu and She-Hulk!" I declared and pointed to where I set the stickers down.
Blake walked up closer to the stickers and looked at them.
He turned to Anna and said, "You know I've been learning how to draw too."

"That's awesome," Anna said.

"Why do you like to draw?" Anna asked.

"Drawing clears my head so much. It releases my inner demons and gives me a sense of peace. And I love the feedback on Instagram, especially from other artists," Blake said.

"Yeah, it's definitely a release for me too. Except I want to break into the comic book industry. Being a famous artist has been my dream since I was a teenager. I want to leave my mark on the world and be remembered," Anna said.

"That makes sense," Blake said. "As an artist, you're basically putting pieces of yourself onto paper or onto whatever. I've only been an artist for about a year now, but I've been overwhelmed by the support from my fellow artists. If my art ever gets recognized by the industry, I wouldn't mind doing cover art for Image Comics, especially if I got to do *Spawn* or some other ongoing comic."

"That's good that you've gotten support. *Spawn*, though?" Anna said with a teasing laugh.

"Hell yeah," Blake said with a smirk.

"*Spawn* is okay. I like a lot of horror comics but to me *Spawn* doesn't age well. It's like they were trying too hard to be edgy like so many other '90s comics," Anna said.

"I know what you mean, but I got a lot of nostalgia for it. It's like, I was born in the '90s, so I don't have nostalgia for that decade. But when I was 13, my mom's boyfriend lent me some comic books. Because I told him I'd been reading graphic novels and manga from my school's library. And the books he lent me were *Spawn* comics. They blew my fucking mind," Blake said.

"Fair enough. Can I see some of your artwork?" Anna asked.

"Sure," Blake said. "It's on my Instagram."

Anna pulled her phone out of her pocket.

"What's your name on there?" she asked.

"Well, I have a personal one and an art account. It's kind of hard to type. Let me just type it for you," Blake said.

Anna handed him her phone. Blake typed out his username on Instagram and opened his profile. He then handed the phone back to her. She looked at it and scrolled through Blake's art account.

"This is some good shit," Anna said.

"Thanks," Blake said.

"I'd follow you on here. But I don't really use social media. I deleted all my accounts because of harassment," Anna said.

"Damn, that sucks. Fuck the haters. Is that why you told me before to message you on Etsy?" Blake asked.

"Yeah," Anna confessed. "Social media has caused me nothing but pain. I had to go off the grid."

Anna wasn't clarifying it to Blake at this moment. However, she told me that, more specifically, it was toxic comic book fans who had harassed her online.

"I'm sorry to hear that," Blake said.

"It is what it is," Anna said. I've noticed she likes to say that a lot in conversations.

Anna handed the phone back to Blake and said, "I really dig your drawings, man. Keep it up."

"Thank you. I really appreciate it, especially coming from you. You're an incredible artist and I hope to someday take after your technique. I like how you have a signature style. Even if it's a simple sketch, I can recognize it as yours," Blake said.

Anna flashed a huge smile and said, "Thanks, man. That means a lot."

"No problem. I know how meaningful positive feedback can be. Putting my artwork on Instagram makes me feel more confident in myself. I don't have any problems with Facebook. I just don't trust it. But on Instagram, I've met so many other artists," Blake said.

"You know why you're good at it? You were born with it. It was always there. It just took a little more time to develop," Anna said.

"Yeah, maybe I was born with it. Once I developed my skill, I didn't stop. I am mostly just self-taught. I didn't take an art class in high school or anything," Blake said.

Anna had an inquisitive look on her face. There was a pause in the conversation before Anna asked Blake another question.

"Have you ever felt like you've lost so much, and the only thing left that matters is art?" Anna asked.

Blake looked surprised by the question.

"No. I can't say I have," he answered.

"Oh, okay. Well, not always, but sometimes, that's exactly how I feel. And when I do, I make the best art," Anna said.

"Well, like I said, for me, it's mostly stress relief. But I don't think higher stress levels means I make better art," Blake said.

Anna nodded.

"Not to pick your brain too much but I'm a little curious. Why do you call yourself a 'proud blerd'?" Anna asked, referring to Blake's Instagram bio.

"Well, I'm proud to be Black and I'm proud to be a nerd," Blake said. "To me, being a blerd is all about being yourself. I first got into comics in the library in junior high. I read manga and graphic novels while my friends played Yu-Gi-Oh. Back in the day, it wasn't cool to be a Black guy who liked anime or comic books. It's not like how it is now. It's more accepted these days. But I remember how it used to be and I'm proud of myself. I don't apologize for it."

Anna nodded and said, "I feel that."

Chapter 4

"All I'm saying is that 'with great power comes great responsibility' is kind of bullshit," David said. "With great power comes crooked, greedy assholes who think they can do whatever they want witout consequences. There's no one like Spider-Man in the real world. Those with great power are like the Kingpin or Lex Luthor with no exception."

A week had passed since David was trying to get what you might call two "normies," Josh and Dezi, to care about indie, horror comic books.

Like every Wednesday, the new weekly comic books were in customers' subscription boxes and for sale on the wall. Like many Wednesdays, David was standing near the register and on another one of his rants.

Nerds ranting is nothing out of the ordinary at Galaxy's Comics & Games. David has listened to me rant me many times too – both at the shop and when we hang out on Monday nights. With all the times he's listened to me talk about the intricate details of the history of Disney Animation, I'm more than willing to hear him out on this.

"I feel like you're talking about people who seek power though," I replied. "Spider-Man doesn't want power. In fact, it's a burden he'd rather do without. If only that's how society worked – the people who don't actually want power are the only ones who get to wield it."

Blake walked up to the counter from the gaming tables in the back of the store. He had already said "hi" to David and Foggy when they first got here, but then went back to playing Yu-Gi-Oh. It now looked like he was in between card games and joining in on the conversation.

David always loves to see Blake. Not just because of the conversations but because Blake will sometimes buy the ob-scure comic books he recommends. While Blake's been reading Manga and superhero comics for more than a decade, he's only recently been getting into indie American comics outside of the "big two" publishers, Marvel and DC.

"Did someone say 'Spider-Man'?" Blake asked. "Y'all know I love Spider-Man."

"Spider-Man is my favorite hero," David said. "I love how he's a dorky guy with a shitty job and bad luck. Anyone can be a hero, you know? Spider-Man always does what he believes is right. These are the people I admire in the real world."

"Isn't your hero Bernie Sanders?" Foggy said after looking up from the Magic: The Gathering binder he was flipping through.

David laughed and said, "No, my hero is you when you shut up and watch the movie."

Unphased by their friendly banter, Blake continued with what he wanted to say.

"My favorite superhero is Static Shock. But I love Spidey too, especially Miles Morales," Blake said.

"Why?" David asked.

"Well, when you think about it, Static is kind of like DC's Spider-Man. They crack jokes. They're not really copy-and-paste kind of heroes. They're not Boy Scouts like Superman or Captain America," Blake said.

"Wait, hold on. What do you mean by 'boy scout'? Your friendly neighborhood Spider-Man will do things like help a kid get home when his bicycle breaks down. And so does Superman in Metropolis. That's one of the things I love about those characters," David said.

"I mean, Supes and Cap feel a little fake to me. Nobody's that polite unless they're putting on a front. That's how I feel about it. But I do like a hero that always does the right thing," Blake said.

"That's kind of why I like Wolverine and the Punisher. They're not copy-and-paste," Foggy said, chiming in.

"Phoebe Bridgers' *Punisher*?" David asked teasingly, referring to a musician he likes who I've been told made an album titled *Punisher*.

"No, motherfucker. The guy with the skull symbol and the big guns," Foggy said. "It's cool to see a gritty anti-hero. And maybe I have a bit of '90s nostalgia."

"Anti-heroes aren't really my thing, but I'm okay with them," I said. "I want to see superheroes saving people. And honestly, that's part of why I'm tired of superhero deconstruction, especially with the conclusion always being 'superheroes are bad'. That doesn't have to be the conclusion. I have no interest in *The Boys,* but I did like *Invincible*. It was a superhero deconstruction, but it was still pro-superhero."

"Yeah, man, and at this point, it's starting to feel like 'what if Superman went bad?' is becoming more cliché than the traditional story of him being a genuinely good guy who is incorruptible. I'm sick of it," David said.

"I agree," I said.

"And anyway, *Watchmen* did the superhero deconstruction thing the best. Nothing will ever compete or compare," David continued. "Alan Moore is the man. As I've said before, I pray upon the book of *Watchmen*," David said half-jokingly.

Blake laughed.

Watchmen is one of the books in the 1980s that brought in the Modern Age of comic books. The book's writer, Alan Moore, is known for being an outspoken anarcho-communist – as he made even more clear in another famous book of his, *V For Vendetta*. The slogan and tagline for *Watchmen*, "who watches the watchmen?" has often been interpreted as not just a critique of superheroes but the inherent contradictions of both law enforcement and power in general. It's one of David's favorite books.

"I like *Watchmen*, but I'm a bigger fan of the zany Silver Age superhero comics that came before it. They're just more fun," I said.

I didn't say it. Because even among friends, I can be nervous to say it. However, this zaniness is the same reason why I love newer comic books like *Squirrel Girl* and *Ms. Marvel*. How can you not love a comic with narration that makes fun of itself and covers of a college girl dressed like a squirrel saying "Nuts!"? That's why it's ironic to me that these books get tons of hate by supposedly traditionally minded, comic book guys online. They say it's for a "newer audience" that doesn't exist. But honestly, half the reason why I enjoy it so much is because it feels like a 1950s and 1960s throwback.

"I'm gonna be honest with you, I've never read *Watchmen*," Blake admitted. "But I fucking love *God Loves, Man Kills*. Not too many comics speak to me like that one does. Chris Claremont is the man."

"Yeah, he is," David said. "Stan Lee claims credit for making *X-Men* about Civil Rights and the mutants as an allegory for the oppressed or marginalized, but really it was Claremont. Have you guys actually read Stan Lee and Jack Kirby's *X-Men* comics before Claremont took over in the '70s? Magneto was just an evil supervillain. He was no Malcolm X."

"You're pronouncing it wrong," Foggy said without even looking up from the Magic: The Gathering binder.

"Pronouncing what wrong?" David asked.

Foggy looked up from the binder of Magic singles and matter-of -factly said, "it's pronounced mag-net-oh not mag-neet-oh."

"Fuck off. You grew up on the '90s cartoon too," David replied.

Foggy just smirked.

"Magnets are neato!" I said.

"How do they work?" Foggy asked with another grin before looking back down at the binder of Magic cards.

"Another thing about the X-Men before Chris Claremont took over – they were all white," Blake said, continuing with what he wanted to talk about. "It's kind of weird that if Stan Lee wanted this to be about racism, why were they all white?"

"Yeah, it's almost as if King Thief is a liar," David said. I impulsively scanned the comic shop to see if any other customers were in the shop. But it was still just these guys and a few gamers playing Yu-Gi-Oh on the back tables.

Blake laughed and said, "Yeah, I know you're a Jack Kirby fanboy. I'll give you that Stan Lee was a credit hog, but I still respect the hell out of him for what he did. I was just saying that Chris Claremont is the man. He not only created the version of the characters we know and love, but he understood that representation mattered."

David nodded and said, "Yeah, it does. Diversity in comics is good because the real world is diverse. Fiction should reflect that."

"True. And it can really mean something to the fans," Blake said. "You know, I first found out about there being a Black Spider-Man when I was 13. My mom showed us a newspaper about a Black, teenage Spider-Man, and I was amazed. At first, I thought she meant 'black suit' Spider-Man but nope."

"Did you know that Miles Morales is inspired by Brian Michael Bendis' kids? He's a Jewish white man who adopted two Black daughters," David said.

"I didn't know that. That's interesting," Blake said.

"He's also said that Riri Williams is specifically based on one of his daughters," David said.

Blake is far from clueless about it, but he doesn't get into the behind-the-scenes stuff of comic books as much as David does. Compared to David or me, Blake doesn't use Twitter, read comic book news or pay a lot of attention to what comic book writers and artists are doing and saying. This doesn't mean he's unaware – far from it. Honestly, it's probably just that he has a healthier relationship with the medium of comics. This is supposed to be entertainment after all.

"Of course, these characters aren't literally his kids. It's fiction. But writing characters loosely based on real people probably makes them feel a lot more real," Blake said.

"Yeah, it's kind of like the creative writing I've been dabbling in lately. I'm super busy with work but my story is slowly but surely coming along. It's based on my job," David said before letting out a dry laugh.

"Hey man, it's like they say, write what you know," Blake said.

"Yep. I mean, hell knows I wouldn't write a romance novel. I've only been in one long-term relationship my entire life," David said.

"Damn. I've never even been in any relationship that lasted more than a few months. I probably wouldn't write a romance comic either," Blake said.

As far as I know, even if Blake loves to draw, he's never written a comic book before. Galaxy's doesn't have any of Blake's artwork displayed like Anna's. I've never even physically seen Blake's artwork in person before. I've only seen the posts on his Instagram account and pictures of his drawings in person at the shop.

"You thinking about writing a comic, Blake?" I asked.

"Maybe. It's on my bucket list," Blake answered.

"That's awesome," David said. "I'll be sure to support it if you do."

"Thanks, bro," Blake said.

"Of course, man. Keep me posted," David said.

"So, the story you're writing is based on your job? You work at a legal aid office, right?" Blake asked.

"Yeah, I'm a lawyer like Matt Murdock. Like him, I wanted to do the right thing and never sacrifice my values. Honestly, in my view, almost every rich motherfucker seeking a lawyer is up to no good. But my clients are poor people, for the most part. Sometimes listening to them talk about their lives and struggles inspires me to write," David said.

"That's commendable. But Spider-Man is your favorite hero? Not the guy who inspired your career?" Blake asked.

David laughed and said, "Yeah, I guess so. I mean, I love Daredevil too."

During the entirety of this conversation, not one other customer walked in the store. There were a few gamers in the back playing Yu-Gi-Oh, but no one else came in.

Galaxy's Comics & Games is a small shop with a loyal customer base. It's not Mile High Comics in Denver, Graham Crackers Comics in Chicago or Midtown Comics in New York. It's not like the bigger comic shops that have booths at conventions. No, Galaxy's is a little hole-in-the-wall store. Many of those who shop here are comic book customers with pull lists. They're also gamers who hang out at the gaming tables in the back and buy snacks, cards and gaming supplies. Because Galaxy's is in a walkable shopping district, every day there are new potential customers coming in and browsing the store. These browsers may even outnumber the regulars. However, they're not where most of the sales numbers come from.

This is part of why conversations like these happen. Regular customers become friends with each other. Because there are never too many strangers around, the shop becomes a safe space for regulars to express what's on their mind without judgment. You can rant about a comic book reboot that's irritating or angering you. You can rave about a new movie you love. You can even talk about current events, other hobbies or your personal life. Regulars get into healthy debates with other nerds who are just as passionate as they are. In short, this is a place where you can be yourself. We let you discover yourself as a comic book nerd.

It's all good here at Galaxy's Comics & Games. This is more than just a store. We're a community. And inside these walls, you don't have to worry about a thing.

Chapter 5

It was around 6:00 PM on another Wednesday. The shop closed in about two hours. David came here with Foggy to pick up his subscriptions. But today, Foggy didn't stick around to look at the Magic: The Gathering singles like he usually does. Instead, he left almost immediately to pick up a pizza. Him and David were going to share it on their weekly movie night tonight.

Right before Foggy left, David and Foggy discussed how they were splitting the money for the pizza. Foggy suggested David sending him the money on PayPal. However, David said he'd been banned from the platform. They eventually agreed on another payment processor. However, Blake was around for this conversation. He questioned David about why and how he was banned from PayPal.

"My last PayPal transaction was sent to me from a *Zombie Tramp* collector on Facebook. He sent me money to pick up some convention exclusives and ship it to him," David said. "It was fucking bullshit. I've done nothing to break the terms of service. I was mostly just using it for buying and selling comic books online."

"Wait, wait, hold on, *Zombie Tramp*? Maybe they thought you were a sex worker? Bro, you know OnlyFan girls be getting banned from PayPal," Blake said.

Foggy laughed. He had a huge smirk on his face. David looked frustrated with the question, but still like he was having a good time.

"Goddammit, Blake!" David said before laughing as well.

"No, PayPal doesn't think I'm a sex worker," David said. "A bunch of people in comic book groups on Facebook sent me money to mail them some con exclusives. I think if you have too many PayPal transactions all at once, PayPal's algorithm automatically bans you. They assume some kind of identity theft or scamming is going on. Or at least they do if you're sending or receiving money from individuals and small businesses instead of large corporations."

"So, you're telling me that if I PayPal a comic shop to buy a variant cover, they might ban me. But if I PayPal a company like eBay or Uber, they'll leave me alone? That's messed up," Blake said.

"Yes, that's exactly what I'm saying," David replied. Shortly after Foggy left, the door of the comic shop opened again. It made its usual ringing sound to alert me to a new customer.

"Hello, welcome to Galaxy's Comics and Games," I said.

"Oh, hi, Anna," I then said after noticing who it was.

Anna walked up to Blake and David.

"What's up, guys?" she said to them.

She then turned to me and said, "I'm just here to pick up my pull."

"You're here early?" Blake said, referring to how she usually doesn't get here until at least 7 p.m. or shortly before closing time.

"Yeah, I'm starting a new art project tonight. But I really wanted to get that new Buffyverse book," Anna said.

I looked at the shelf behind me, went through the alphabetized names on the cardboard sheet dividers until I found Anna's "pull list box." She only had one comic she hadn't bought yet. It was the new issue of *The Vampire Slayer*. That's an alternate universe *Buffy the Vampire Slayer* story where Willow is the "chosen one" and the slayer instead of Buffy.

I turned back around and handed the comic book to Anna. "Sweet!" she said before setting it down on the counter to purchase.

"How is that book?" David asked. "I only read the first issue, but I was thinking about getting the trade."

"I love it," Anna said with a huge smile. "Willow is bae." I didn't actually ring her up for her purchase yet. Because it looked like she might be having a conversation first. Anna doesn't see David very often. Usually, he and Foggy are gone before Anna gets here on Wednesday nights.

"Hell yeah," David said. His eyes were lighting up. "I grew up on *Buffy*. In middle school and high school, it was on every Tuesday night, and I never missed an episode. I still consider it my favorite show."

"Same," Anna said. "I know I'm younger than you, but I grew up on *Buffy* too. I first watched it on Netflix in high school. It spoke to me. The fact that anyone could be a slayer – even me. And then an untrained, unprepared girl reluctantly became the greatest slayer in history. I ate that shit up."

"That's awesome. I'm not gonna lie, *Buffy* was half the reason I first signed up for Netflix back in the day," David said. James, one of the gamers who had been playing Yu-Gi-Oh at the tables in the back of the store, walked up to the counter.

"A-yo, Blake, you're up," James said.

"Cool, cool," Blake said. He fist bumped Anna and David

and said, "I'll catch you guys later." He then walked to the gaming tables in the back of the store.

"Do you read a lot of horror comics? It seems like every time I see you, you're buying another horror comic," David asked.

"I sure do," Anna said.

"What are some of your favorites?" David asked.

Anna paused and thought about it.

"Well, *Afterlife with Archie* is up there," she said. "But I love all the Buffyverse stuff. Those were the first comics I ever had in my pull list."

"Hell yeah! *Afterlife with Archie* is one of my favorites too. You know, I have a commission at home of Zombie Jughead. Erica Henderson drew it for me," David said.

He showed Anna a picture of the commission on his phone.

Anna smiled and said, "That's so fucking cool. Yeah, the art in that book is amazing. I love a good, bloody, horror story. Characters in horror are important to me, too. But bloodshed is essential."

David laughed, put his phone back in his pocket and said, "*Buffy* isn't that gory though."

Anna smirked and replied, "Yeah, well, it was network TV in the late '90s and early 2000s. By that standard, *Buffy* was gruesome. It's about murderous demons and blood-sucking vampires. Anyway, like I said, the best horror is about the characters. And I'll always love the characters in *Buffy* and *Angel*."

"Yeah, they're great. But I think the best horror is allegorical – like how the demons Buffy fought were often a metaphor for her internal demons. A horror story should say something about the real world. Great art speaks truth to power. And to me, *Buffy* did that. As I'm assuming you're aware, the first same-sex kiss on network TV was on *Buffy the Vampire Slayer*," David said.

Anna frowned and said, "People say that, but you know that's not actually true."

"Huh? What isn't?" David asked.

"The first same sex kiss on network TV was not on *Buffy*. Two women kissed on *LA Law* on NBC in 1991," Anna said. David said nothing. He just stared silently at Anna in disbelief.

"Look, I'll show ya," Anna said.

Anna pulled out her phone and typed something on it. She then showed the screen to David. He was now staring in disbelief at her phone. But this time it looked more like the first stage of grief than legitimate skepticism.

"Hold on, Anna," I said. "I've never actually seen an episode of *Buffy*. I'm not really a horror fan like you guys. But I thought the first same-sex kiss was on *Buffy*."

"No, it wasn't. Look," Anna said before handing me her phone.

I looked at it. There was a picture of two women kissing. The headline read, "Today in Gay History: *LA Law*'s Lesbian Kiss." And what do you know? The first same-sex kiss on Network TV wasn't on the beloved horror program, *Buffy the Vampire Slayer*. It was on some legal drama from the early 1990s.

I handed the phone back to her and teasingly said, "Well, someone's world was just shattered" before looking at David.

He didn't appear amused.

"Look, David," Anna said. "No one's a bigger *Buffy* fan than me. This isn't even the first time I've had this conversation. That's why I had that article bookmarked on my phone! I still think *Buffy* is a big deal. The kiss on *LA Law* wasn't between two of the main characters. It wasn't part of an ongoing relation-ship like Willow and Tara. When Willow and Tara kissed, it was part of a prominent, ongoing subplot. It wasn't just a one-episode thing."

David looked like he was feeling a little better.

He nodded and said, "That makes sense."

"Plus, when I was a teenager, seeing Willow fall in love with a woman after being with Oz – that meant a lot to me," Anna said. "Even if I first saw it in the 2010s and not the 2000s, it was the first time I felt like I'd seen something like that. It gave me confidence as a bisexual person."

"That's awesome. I'm glad it could do that for you," David said.

"Yeah, and it didn't hurt that the actresses on *Buffy* and *Angel* were fucking hot. I watched that shit and was like, yeah, I like girls for sure," Anna said.

David let out a loud and surprisingly long laugh.

"You laughed a little too hard at that," I said teasingly.

"Sarah Michelle Gellar was my first celebrity crush," David admitted.

"Nice. Good call," Anna said.

Chapter 6

"What's so allegorical about *Afterlife with Archie*, though? You said horror should be allegorical and that's one of your favorites." Anna said.

David's eyes lit up.

"Well, I think you have to put that comic in the context of the time it came out," David said.

"What do you mean?" Anna asked.

"Well, *Afterlife with Archie* was published before *Riverdale* was on the CW. It was before Archie had many other comics featuring edgier, more 'mature' versions of the characters. Riverdale U.S.A was supposed to represent middle America, and everything traditionally considered to be wholesome. And what better way for Archie Comics to reinvent itself than by zombies rampaging through Riverdale and killing everybody?"

"Makes sense," I said, chiming in.

"So… What? Are you saying the zombies in *Afterlife with Archie* were essentially 'killing' traditional, family values?" Anna asked.

"Hell yeah," David replied. "Archie was re-inventing itself as a progressive publisher. They had a same-sex marriage on the cover of *Life with Archie #16*. And remember, this was the same year that DC wouldn't let Batwoman get married."

"I remember," Anna said.

"Right. But over at Archie Comics, Riverdale wasn't an idyllic 1950s-esque town anymore. Even in the so-called 'classic' style Archie stories, Riverdale became a fantasy world where Kevin was gay and everyone in town accepted him. In the beautiful town of Riverdale, the jock, Moose, was now best friends with the nerd, Dilton," David said.

"Homophobia was very real in *Afterlife with Archie*, though. That's why Ginger and Nancy were sneaking around playing 'Brokeback Riverdale' as one of them put it," Anna said.

"Sure. But *Afterlife with Archie* was a dark and grim horror comic. In that version of the characters, Veronica and Jughead hate each other, and Reggie is a literal sociopath," David said.

"So, it's more grounded," I said.

"Yeah, exactly," David said. "*Afterlife with Archie* is supposed to be a realistic horror story. It's not silly and campy like *Archie vs. Predator*, for instance. It's certainly not a feel-good Archie story in their more traditional style."

"I like both realistic and campy horror stories," Anna said.

"I do too," David said. "And *Buffy* always had a little of both, didn't it?"

Anna nodded and said, "It did."

"But my point with *Afterlife with Archie* is that after it was released, Archie's publishing line was never the same. Riverdale was still an idyllic town in the cartoony, feel-good stories. But it was more like a utopia that we should work towards. The 1950s nostalgia was dead. And those damn zombies in *Afterlife with Archie* delivered the final nail in that coffin."

"Maybe. So, why was Jughead the first to die in that book? Do you think there's any symbolism in that?" Anna asked.

"Well, technically, it was Jughead's dog who died first. And yes, I do think there was symbolism in Hot Dog dying first. What could be more innocent and wholesome than Jughead's dog?" David said.

Blake had now walked back to the front of the store.

"That was quick," I said to Blake.

"Yeah, I didn't actually finish the game. It's time to head home though. I'll see James again next week," Blake said, referring to one of the other regular Yu-Gi-Oh players at Galaxy's.

Having overheard part of the conversation, Blake turned to David and Anna and said, "I haven't read what you guys are talking about. But I'm just glad the Black guy isn't always the first to die in horror movies anymore."

David laughed and said, "Yeah, that trope does seem to be a thing of the past now."

"And I'm glad! Honestly, I'd rather the Black guy not die at all. I mean, Black men in America have gone through some shit. We're survivors like the final girl. Why not show that in a horror movie?" Blake said.

"That's a point," Anna said. David nodded.

"Anyway, I'll catch y'all later. I got to get something to eat," Blake said.

"Yeah, I got some shit to do too. A starving artist never sleeps," Anna said.

"So, you're ready to check out?" I asked her.

"Yeah, I'm just buying this today," Anna said before picking the comic book up off the counter and then setting it back down.

Blake waved as he walked out of the door. I rang up Anna and she left the store as well.

David began to browse books on the wall. He did this as he

waited for Foggy to get back with the pizza that he ordered for their movie night.

Three gamers, James, Brian and Robert, continued to play Yu-Gi-Oh in the back tables. I don't know all the gamers' names, but I knew theirs. They're good guys. They occasionally buy cards and gaming supplies. They often buy snacks from Galaxy's when hanging out here.

The door of the shop opened. It rang as it did.

"Welcome to Galaxy's Comics and Games," I said.

A person dressed in a Ghostface costume walked in the door. A Ghostface costume is what the killers in the *Scream* movies wear. However, this costume was unlike any Ghostface costume I'd ever seen before. It had pieces of worn black fabric that appeared to have been sewn on by someone. And the costume had several noticeable burn marks on it. There were burn marks on the mask and even more on the sleeves.

However, the biggest departure from a more typical Ghostface costume was the weapon they were holding. It wasn't a hunting knife. It was what looked to be a very real chainsaw. It had a yellow base and a black handle. The blades looked old and rusty.

This isn't the first time I've seen someone dress up like a character from comic books, video games or movies. In fact, on Free Comic Book Day, we offer additional free comics to anyone who shows up in cosplay. But surely, no one would bring a real chainsaw into a comic book store, right? Hell, if this were a convention, you wouldn't be able to get past security with a real hunting knife – much less a chainsaw.

David turned his head to the left and looked at the Ghostface cosplayer. He had an *Invincible Red Sonja* comic book in his hand that he'd been flipping through.

"Cool costume. I love *Scream*," David said somewhat loudly from across the room.

The Ghostface cosplayer slowly walked toward David without replying. He started to look nervous now. Personally, I was getting extremely peeved.

"Hey, man," I said. "Those aren't real blades, are they?"

The Ghostface cosplayer took another step towards David. And then another step. David put the comic book back on the wall and began to step back. This Ghostface cosplayer was now just a few feet away from him.

"Do I know you?" David asked.

Without warning, the Ghostface cosplayer went from walking slowly to bolting forward. The sudden shift in movement caused David to trip and fall backwards, dropping the comic book in the process.

"This ain't cosplay, bitch. I just wanted to kill ya like they do in the movies," the chainsaw wielder said. It was Ghostface's voice. They must've had a voice modulating device on them.

Rrrrrrnnn. Rrrrnnnnn. Bvvvzzzttt.

The chainsaw was definitely real. This Ghostface wannabe had turned it on.

"Hey!" I screamed.

It all happened so fast. It was a total blur. Before I could process what was happening, David was a bloody mess on the floor. The chainsaw had sliced him to pieces.

Chapter 7

"Pathetic, starry-eyed fanboys act like the comic shop is a wonderful, magical, happy-go-lucky place. But no one is even here! That guy I disposed of – was he the only customer who was actually buying a comic book?" the masked maniac asked.

The chainsaw was no longer roaring. Because of the killer's voice modulator, I continued to hear Ghostface's voice from the *Scream* movies.

At this point, James, Robert and Brian had gotten up from their chairs. They didn't even stop to pick up their Yu-Gi-Oh cards. They just left them on the gaming tables and started fleeing. They were bolting towards the back exit door.

I was stunned and frozen in place behind the cash register. I felt as if I were floating. I wasn't only an onlooker at the scene. It was like I was observing my own body. I had no control. I could only watch myself as I stood there stuck.

"Woke SJWs are ruining what used to be a great hobby! Well, fuck that bullshit. It's time to make comics great again!" the maniacal monster screamed before revving back up the chainsaw.

Rrrrrrnnn. Rrrrnnnnn. Bvvvzzzttt.

As the Yu-Gi-Oh players ran, the killer walked slowly behind them.

I remained paralyzed. As the chainsaw rumbled, it felt like every bone in my body was shaking. The concept of passing time was no longer real. Everything felt like an incoherent blur of madness as I waited for this horrible experience to be over.

I keep the back door unlocked whenever the store is open. But even if it were locked, it unlocks from the inside. So, exiting through it shouldn't be a problem.

The back door is technically in a much smaller room, but you don't have to open a door to enter this room. You essentially walk through a door-sized gap. After doing this, in front of you is the exit door, on your left side is the bathroom and on your right side is a storage room. The storage space was currently locked by me, but the bathroom door wasn't.

James was the first to reach the back door.

"This way. Let's go!" he screamed.

But when James tried to open the door, it didn't budge.

"What the hell?" James exclaimed. He continued to struggle, furiously turning the doorknob back and forth. The nob turned all the way to each side, but the door didn't move.

Robert shoved him and yelled, "Dude, just unlock it."

James no longer had his hand on the door. Robert did now. He twisted the doorknob's lock back and furth repeatedly. After every turn, he tried to open the door again and failed each time.

"Something must be blocking it on the outside!" Robert yelled.

"Yeah, no shit, Sherlock," Brian said.

The chainsaw wielder was now only a few yards away from them. They turned off the chainsaw and began to talk into the voice changing device again.

"Cultural Marxist writers and fans don't even care if comic books sell or not. They think they're activists. But comics are supposed to be a business," the killer said before revving up the chainsaw again.

Rrrrrrnnn. Rrrrnnnnn. Bvvvzzzttt.

"Well, up yours, woke moralists! Cancel this!" the killer screamed.

The Ghostface wannabe lifted the chainsaw up over their head and dropped it down like a hammer. After hitting the top of his head, the chainsaw went through the middle of Robert's skull. Blood splattered onto James and Brian who were standing next to him.

James and Brian didn't try to fight the killer. They were standing next to the bathroom by the exit, but they didn't enter it. I'm assuming they figured that facing up against a chainsaw, they'd be trapped and goners inside. Instead, while the killer massacred their friend, Brian and Robert sprinted towards the front entrance. As they ran in my direction, I remained frozen in shock.

"Comics aren't even fun anymore. Activist rants aren't fun to read. But you know what is fun? I'll show ya!" the killer screamed.

James and Brian didn't get far. The killer took a few steps forward and swung the chainsaw like a baseball bat. It hit Brian somewhere in the stomach, slicing him in half. On the same swing, the chainsaw struck James in the lower torso.

The blood-soaked bodies fell to the floor. The killer turned off the lumbering chainsaw.

"Fuck yeah! Is this what they mean by killing two birds with one stone? Slice one and get another free. I mean, both these guys are half off," the maniac said.

The Ghostface costume was now covered in blood – as was much of Galaxy's Comics & Games.

The killer began walking in my direction, but I remained immobile. It felt like I was stuck. Because this couldn't be real, could it? Am I watching a movie? Is this a bad dream?

When the killer reached the cash register, they didn't even turn towards me. They just continued to walk on by. The Ghostface wannabe didn't even look at me. They were looking at the door.

"A-A-Adrian? Is that you?" I asked as I stared at the burned, bloody Ghostface mask.

Now the killer turned their head towards me.

"Adrian?" I asked again.

The Ghostface wannabe continued to stare at me without saying a word. I don't know for how long. Throughout this ordeal, time wasn't just standing still but was a meaningless relic.

"Sorry about the mess," the killer said. They turned their head back towards the front door and walked out of it.

Chapter 8

I suffer from night terrors. When I sleep, I dream about all the worst things that can happen in my life – like the shop I own going out of business or my parents dying. Other times, what I dream about aren't surface-level or even remotely logical fears. They can feel worse because, unlike dreams that involve real worries of mine, the whole world is a darker place in these dreams. The people I love will say the words of my biggest enemies. I lose all my strengths and I become irreparably hindered by my weaknesses. No one behaves like themselves. Instead, everyone around me behaves like the same monster tormenting me. I'm alone in these dreams. It's just me against the world. It's a place where nothing has worked out and I can count on no one for anything – not even myself.

When I have dreams like this, I wake up screaming.

My night terrors are rarely violent. I don't "dream about cutting off heads with a shovel" like that one Insane Clown Posse song. I don't dream about being victimized with a shovel either. But nonetheless, these dreams feel like what I imagine the final girl must feel like near the end of a slasher flick – terror, loneliness and devastation.

The final girl stands alone against the masked, blade-wielding killer. All her friends have been killed but she remains.

She might have tears in her eyes, but she still stands tall. She is relentless and refuses to die. She does what she needs to do to survive. She will cut through the rope to escape from where the killer has trapped her. She will jump out the closed window of a two-story building and let the glass shards pierce her flesh. She will do everything in her power to persevere. Because the final girl must live another day. There's still a whole world out there away from the killer and away from this horrible place he has forever tainted. She must escape and arrive at her next destination. Because life is worth living, God dammit. She's gone through too much to let some psychopathic maniac end her story prematurely. She is stronger than this. She is stronger than him. That's why she is the only survivor.

Who am I in the slasher movie? I'm pretty sure I'm the nerdy guy or the stoner who gets killed sometime in the second act – or as *Cabin in the Woods* called this character archetype, "the fool." I don't think I have the fortitude of the final girl. When I'm battling demons in my sleep, if it gets too much, all I need to do is wake up from the nightmare. But the final girl at the end of a slasher flick? She truly has to beat this monster. In her fight for survival, she has to win. And she uses all her might and wits to do it.

This is something I've talked to Anna about. She thinks I could survive a slasher flick. Because I'm a pop culture nerd and I know and understand all the "rules" of surviving the killer's rampage – such as don't have sex, don't do drugs, don't split up and never say "I'll be right back." She has a point. Not breaking these rules might be how I'd survive the *Scream* movies. However, the *Scream* movies are a meta commentary on the genre. In most slasher flicks, the characters not only don't know they're in a movie, but they have no reason to believe the killer is following horror movie logic.

I sat at home staring at the TV. Images of Harley Quinn, Poison Ivy and King Shark flashed back at me, but I wasn't listening or comprehending anything. It's a Monday night and David should be hanging out with me on my one day off like he always is. But he's not here. David isn't watching the show with me. Because a masked killer with a chainsaw ended his life, like something straight out of a slasher flick.

Ever since I witnessed four people get murdered, my night terrors have not only worsened but become guaranteed like gravity. While they used to be more occasional, I've had them every night since. And for the first time, my night terrors have started to become violent too.

Even if today weren't a Monday, my one day of the week off, Galaxy's Comics & Games is temporarily closed by order of the local police. It's a crime scene. No civilian is allowed to go inside the comic shop until whatever they're investigating is finished.

Bzzt. Bzzt.

My phone sat on the coffee table in front of me. It was on Silent Mode, but I heard the vibrations of a new text message I'd received. I reached over and grabbed my phone. It was Anna. She had sent me an article from a local newspaper. The headline read "Four Dead in Massacre at Comic Shop." This article was accompanied with a text from Anna that simply said, "WTF?"

I'd already read the article. In fact, I'm quoted in it. A local journalist talked to me after it happened.

Even though I was one of the primary sources the reporter used in the article, I still learned something from reading it. Apparently, whoever killed those people used a simple, wooden doorstop to prevent the back door from opening. From the outside, the killer stuck one under the closed door. This sneaky trick practically "locked" the door so the victims couldn't escape.

After finding out about this, I read online that enough brute force should've been able to open the door – like kicking or body slamming oneself into it. But I guess in their panicked state, James, Brian and Robert didn't think to do that. Instead, they turned around and ran back in the direction of the front door and the deranged killer.

I texted Anna back, "Yep, David's funeral arrangements are on Wednesday."

I looked at what I just sent and thought about it. This may have sounded insensitive. I mean, I'm pretty sure I'm traumatized for life so maybe people should cut me some slack right now. Nonetheless, I don't want to make it sound like David was the only one of the four killed who I cared about. David was one of my best friends, but it pains me thinking about what happened to all those guys.

Also, maybe Anna was interested in the funeral arrangements of the other three. I know Anna knew David but I'm not sure if she knew the three Yu-Gi-Oh players. Often, I'm not paying a lot of attention to what's happening at the gaming tables. However, I'm assuming Anna knew at least one of them. She didn't play card games or Dungeons & Dragons at the store, but she did often hang out at the gaming tables and draw in her sketchbook.

Upon reflection, I then sent another text. It said, "Let me know if you want the info on that… or the others who died." Anna replied with "Yeah, text me about David's funeral" and another text that said, "can I call?" I texted back, "yes."

The phone rang immediately afterwards. I picked it up.

"Hey," I said.

"Hey there," Anna replied. "How are you feeling?"

I didn't know how to respond. There was a pause.

"If you don't want to talk about it, I understand," Anna said.

Disregarding the last statement, I said, "I can't believe I'm alive. I don't feel like I deserve to be here. Why did I get to survive?"

Family members have said my autism is why I'm so honest. Maybe. But at this moment, I really did need to talk to someone.

"That's tough," Anna said. "I'm here for you, you know."

"Yeah, I know," I replied.

There was another pause. I have no idea for how long. Since the killings, I've lost much of my conception of time.

"So, what's gonna happen to Galaxy's Comics and Games?" Anna said, breaking the silence.

I struggled with the previous question because I didn't know how to put my thoughts into words. But this question genuinely stumped me.

"What do you mean?" I asked.

"Like, are you gonna permanently close the doors?" Anna asked.

There was another pause.

"Honestly, I hadn't even thought about that," I told her. "Probably not, though. Right now, the store is shut down by police order. It's a crime scene. They got the tape on it and everything. Even I can't go inside."

"Why do they think the killer did it?" Anna asked.

"Who?" I asked.

"The police," she said.

"Oh. I don't know. They haven't told me," I said.

There was another pause in the conversation. I hope Anna isn't thinking there's something wrong with me. I already have a developmental disability that specifically affects the way I communicate. And watching my friend and three other customers die last week hasn't exactly helped.

"I sympathize with what you're going through," Anna said. "I wasn't close to David like you were. But I get it. I never told you this, but my dad was killed. Or at least cancer killed him. Brain cancer. It was extremely fast. He died just months after his diagnosis."

"I'm sorry to hear that," I replied.

"It's okay. It was a long time ago. Your shit is new though. You have my sympathy," Anna said.

Without skipping a beat, Anna said, "I don't think you should shut down the store. My dad was in the hospital for a while, but then he had at-home hospice care. In his last days, I read *Calvin and Hobbes* to him on his deathbed. I read the book collections he gave me as a kid. Those *Calvin and Hobbes* books were some of the first comics I ever read. That tumor had him all kinds of fucked up. He drooled a lot and wasn't all there. But he still knew why his daughter was reading this comic to him. And why it was special."

"It sounds like you really loved him," I said.

"Yeah," Anna replied. "And I guess I've always viewed my love for comics as like an extension of that love we had for each other, if that makes any sense."

"It does," I said.

There was another pause before I blurted out a question of my own.

"What if this killer is trying to destroy my shop?" I asked.

"Well, you better not let this asshole win then," Anna said.

Chapter 9

It seems like the image a lot of people have of comic book collections is dusty, old, long boxes in the garage, basement or attic. These dusty boxes are filled with periodicals that no one has read for decades. But many comic book fans have a stack of new, bagged and boarded comic books that they plan on reading soon. This stack of comic books is kept on dressers, coffee tables and nightstands. A wrinkly snapping sound is made when a new comic book is placed on top of it. The comic book fan gobbles down that stack of comic books like a Netflix binge. Sometimes they'll turn the page, and gasp at what's revealed in the splash page that follows.

A typical comic book reader doesn't just like comics but loves comics. They don't read new comic books by turning on a TV and picking something out in a streaming service menu. They keep up to date with all the different comic books that are coming out. They set up subscription services at comic shops such as mine. They make regular visits to their local (or semi-local) comic shop. And then they take home with them the comic books that they bought. They do all of this because the comic book medium means a lot to its readers. A typical comic book reader can't imagine what it would be like to never read another comic. It's like most people can't imagine never watching television again or most bookworms can't imagine never being able to read another book.

Comics are a medium, not a genre. This means it's not only superhero, horror or humor stories. A comic book is just another way to tell a story – any kind of story. It's a storytelling medium like (prose) books, movies or plays. For those movie lovers who enjoy reading, a comic is like the best of both worlds. It may be a visual medium like a movie, but you still read it like you do any other book.

The best comic book is one that, in theory, could be read in less than 15 minutes but instead, you spend at least an hour. You gaze in wonder at the artwork inside the pages of the comic book. You're fully immersed in not just the story but the artist's rendition of it. You take your time gazing lovingly at every single panel. Nowadays, the varying styles of comic book artwork is larger than ever. There's everything from more traditional, simple, comic strip-style drawings to actual paintings.

Reading a comic isn't like reading anything else. Like reading a novel, you give the characters the voice you imagine in your head. But it's still different than reading a novel where you imagine the entire story in your head. However, when reading a comic, you still have to fill in the blanks and imagine exactly what is happening in between panels. Some comics will show very little time span in between panels to convey the panic a character is feeling or the deadly seriousness of a scene. Because when reading the comic, you feel how abnormal it is for every few seconds of the occurrence to show another panel.

Some people like to look at the panel's artwork before reading the dialogue or narration. Others read the words before getting a good look at the drawings (beyond what they might notice in their peripheral vision.) Personally, unless it's a narration, I usually look at the drawing before reading the words. But sometimes, I can't help myself and I'll look at all the drawings on a page before I actually read any of it.

Comic books aren't popular like video games – something that so many people love, it spurred the development of a major video streaming platform. Comics aren't even like prose novels – something that's sold at every airport in the United States. No, comic books are special. The people who read every new issue of a comic book and hold it in their hands visit the inside walls of a comic shop. Almost every American has seen the inside walls of a movie theater. But sadly, very few people have seen inside the walls of a comic shop.

Part of why comic book fans are so passionate about comics is because we're a much smaller audience than people who watch movies, play video games, or even read books. Someone who loves video games probably never has to worry about an end to the video game industry. But for the comic book fan, there's a very real feeling like we must buy from and support the comic book industry every month or every week. Because we don't want this medium we love to die. Those of us who think like this are the Wednesday warriors regularly congregating inside the walls of a comic shop.

They say comic shops are the backbone of the comic book industry. In this day and age, there certainly are other options to read them. You can read them digitally on your tablet. The collected editions of the issues can be read in book collections sold wherever books are sold. Ever since the popularity of superhero movies, more and more public libraries have a large and vibrant graphic novel section. However, the comic shop is the place to be if you want to read the issues as they come out. It's how you keep up with the story many months or even years before the trade paperback or hardcover is released. Or at the very least, it's where you shop if you want to physically hold the comic book in your hand instead of reading it digitally.

Comic shops have a reputation for being musty and cluttered. And I must admit, my little hole-in-the-wall shop doesn't do much to counter this reputation. But the unfortunate truth is that comic shops have also developed a reputation as being a white boys' club or least unwelcoming to outsiders. I do everything I can to break this stigma surrounding comic shops. This isn't just because owning a comic shop is my source of income, and more customers means more business. But also, it's because I want more people to fall in love with this beautiful, messy underdog of a medium.

I've thought a lot about what Anna said to me over the phone. I've realized that Galaxy's Comics & Games is important not only because of the comics and gaming community but because of the comics themselves. I'm doing my part to keep the comic book medium alive.

Anna was at David's funeral. We said "hi" and hugged before the service, but I sat with my family during it. She sat by herself in the back row and left immediately afterwards. Anna didn't stick around to chat with anybody. With everything I was feeling, perhaps I should've done the same, but I felt like I couldn't. I was here to pay my respects. This meant not only saying goodbye to the corpse but talking to the loved ones.

I saw Foggy at David's funeral too. However, other than brief pleasantries, we didn't say much to each other. I got the feeling that he wasn't coming back to Galaxy's without David. This was a shame because I considered him a friend too.

Blake was chattier when I saw him. He asked me, "How are you holding up?" I told him I don't want to talk about it. He said he can't imagine what it must be like to have witnessed what I did. He asked me if there were any triggers that he should know about. "Not that I know of," I told him.

Blake tried to reminisce about good times with David. However, it ended up mostly being him talking about his memories of David and me just listening. Blake told me about a *Transformers* group on Facebook that he and David were in. He said that someone once posted a Casey W. Coller drawing of Optimus Prime "taking a knee" like Colin Kaepernick. Group members complained about the post. David defended the artwork, saying the government on Optimus Prime's home planet is very draconian, and it makes sense that he'd support Black Lives Matter.

"They kept on telling David, 'Shut up. You live in your mom's basement' and he just kept saying, 'Get fucked, bigot' over and over. Nothing else. Just 'get fucked, bigot,' he told them," Blake said while laughing.

Blake was at James's, Robert's and Brian's funerals too, but we didn't talk as much then. Like at David's funeral, I sat with my family during the service. Before and afterwards, I spent much of my time with Blake and the other gamers from Galaxy's Comics & Games. They talked to me, but I said the bare minimum. Again, I mostly just listened.

It's not that I didn't necessarily want to talk to any of them about it. I just never know how to handle funerals – and I especially didn't know how to handle these ones. I felt like people were whispering about me at all four of them. Like, maybe they blamed me for the murders. But fortunately, I never felt this way about Anna, Blake or any of his Yu-Gi-Oh buddies. They were all very warm to me.

David's mom gave me a big hug. However, with many of the other family members of David, James, Brian and Robert, it seemed like there was something they wanted to say to me but couldn't. Some appeared to outright despise me. Maybe it was all in my head. I don't know.

The police allowed me to reopen the shop on Wednesday – exactly seven days after the massacre. However, because of the funerals and the new books I had to organize and put away, I didn't open until the following Tuesday. This means subscribers had gone two weeks without their comics. The first week was because of the police and the second week was because of me.

You'd think maybe that there'd be less customers because they were scared. But my comic book subscribers came to the shop in droves – eager to read what they had missed while Galaxy's had been closed. The gamers were also back in droves. Friday Night Magic was bigger than it had been in months. Everyone was just eager to return to what they'd been missing – even if most were aware of the massacre that happened here. Maybe they'd suspected I might permanently close the shop and they'd never be able to do this at Galaxy's Comics & Games again. Perhaps they were making up for this predicted and imagined lost time as well.

Chapter 10

It was the second Wednesday of Galaxy's Comics & games being open again after two weeks of closure. There was no sign of the Ghostface wannabe returning ever again. In many ways, it was just another Wednesday. At about 7:00 PM, an hour before closing time, Anna stopped by to pick up her books. This was the first time she'd been here since the night of the tragedy.

"Welcome to Galaxy's Comics and Games. Oh, hey, Anna!" I said.

"Hey," she said. She wasn't looking at my face – at least not until she got to the cash register. She wasn't smiling at first. She flashed a pained smile when she asked, "Anything new for me?" referring to her comic book subscriptions.

I turned around and looked at the pull list comic books on the shelf behind me. I found the cardboard divider with her name on it.

"Nope, nothing this week," I said.

"Oh, okay," Anna said.

Just then Blake walked up to the front of the store. He'd been playing Yu-Gi-Oh in the back.

"Hey," he said. Anna nodded.

"I haven't seen you since the funeral," Blake said to her. Huh?

"Blake, that was just a couple weeks ago," I blurted out.

Blake laughed uncomfortably and said, "Yeah, Eric, I know." Even if the laugh was uncomfortable, he smiled like a friend who appreciated my bluntness.

"I guess it's just a thing people say," Blake said.

Anna looked at Blake and nodded.

"You guys can just say it," I blurted out. "You're thinking about the killings that happened here."

Anna looked at Blake and then at me.

"Is it hard to be back here after seeing what you saw?" Anna asked me. Blake appeared startled by the question. Maybe because he asked me something similar at David's funeral, but I didn't really answer him.

"Not really. It's not harder than anywhere else," I answered.

Blake now had a more inquisitive look on his face.

"Eric, man, I'm worried about you," Blake said. "Maybe you should let your parents run the store for a little bit."

My dad is the accountant at Galaxy's. He handles finances and other numbers. My mom often works at the cash register when I'm unavailable. Both help me out on Free Comic Book Day and during other big events.

"Maybe. But I kind of feel like I'm constantly reliving what I saw that night. It doesn't matter where I am. I've spent so much time here over the years. The shop might be my job, but it almost feels like a second home to me. I can't go home and cope. I need to stay here and live my life normally," I said.

I stopped talking. But Blake and Anna just looked at me. I think they were expecting me to vent more. If anything, I surprised myself by how much I did just say.

Breaking the silence, Blake said, "That makes sense, man. Like I told you at the funeral, I'm here for you if you need to talk."

"Thanks," I said.

"We can't let this tragedy define this shop. This place means too much to us for it to be tainted like that. We can't let the terrorists win, so to speak," Anna said.

"I agree. This place is special to a lot of people," Blake said.

"Although I guess it wasn't special to that fuckboy Adrian," Blake added with an angry tone.

I was about to say something about this, but a customer walked in the door.

"Welcome to Galaxy's Comics and Games," I said.

The customer smiled at me. She then moved on to explore the shop.

"Is she a regular?" Anna asked quietly. This customer might have heard Anna say this, but I'm honestly not sure.

"No," I said.

Before this customer walked in the door, it was only me, Anna, Blake and some of the usual gamers in the back of the store. As soon as she walked in, we all just stopped talking about the massacre.

Blake and Anna started chatting about manga and how it compares to western comics. I chimed in occasionally.

The customer who I didn't know eventually made her way to the back issue boxes. She spent about 15 minutes looking through them before coming to the register to check out. She stopped and stood behind Blake and Anna as if she were waiting for them to finish.

"Oh, they're not in line," I said. "They're just my friends."

"Yeah, don't be afraid to shove us out the way!" Blake joked.

The customer laughed and said, "Oh, okay. Yeah, I

should've known. I think there are folks like y'all in every comic shop."

The customer set a stack of what was mostly old *Saga* comic books on the counter. I began to scan them and check her out.

"I'm here on vacation for a wedding. I wanted to check out the local comic shop – and hopefully find some gems in the back issue boxes," the customer said.

"Well, thanks for stopping by. I hope you're happy with what you found," I said.

"I am," the customer replied. "I love *Saga*."
I grabbed a random one of Anna's stickers and put it in the customer's bag. I told her the price and she swiped her debit card to pay.

"Hey, that's my sticker he put in her bag!" Anna said.

"Really? That's so cool." The customer pulled it out and looked at it.

"Yep. And I love your shirt," Anna said, pointing to the customer's black T-shirt with panels from the nonfiction graphic novel, *Fun Home*.

"Thank you," the customer replied. "Alison Bechdel is a hero of mine. I got to represent!"

"Where did you buy it?" Anna asked.

"It's custom. I wanted a *Fun Home* shirt so I could wear it at conventions and stuff, but I couldn't find one for sale anywhere. So, I made it myself," the customer said.

"That's fucking rad," Anna said.

"Thanks," the customer said.

"I'm Anna. What's your name? Do you have an Etsy shop or something?" Anna asked.

"I'm Jennifer. And nope, no Etsy shop. I'm not really a crafter or an artist or anything. Like I said, I just wanted a *Fun*

Home shirt to wear myself," Jennifer said.

Anna pulled out a business card and handed it to her.

"You should check out my Etsy shop! I have a lot more stickers, some prints and original artwork. I deleted my social media but don't be afraid to message me on Etsy," Anna said.

Jennifer looked at the business card and smiled.

"Thanks, I will," she said before putting Anna's business card in with her bag of comics.

"But also, if you want another one of Anna's stickers, you can always come back here. You get one free with every purchase," I said.

"Maybe I will the next time I'm in town," Jennifer said.

"You didn't hear about anything… bad… that happened here, did you?" Blake blurted out.

Seriously, Blake? I know it's ironic for someone with autism to be annoyed by this, but he really has no filter sometimes.

Anna shifted nervously. I imagine I did as well. Jennifer looked confused.

"Huh? No, I didn't," Jennifer said. "What are you talking about?" Jennifer asked.

I felt like I should say something about this. However, I had no idea what I could or should say.

"Never mind," Blake said to Jennifer before looking at me.

"Oh okay," Jennifer said, laughing nervously.

Chapter 11

Foggy stopped by the shop the next day. It was a Thursday, so it wasn't the day I was used to seeing him. He used to come here almost every Wednesday with David and occasionally participated in Friday Night Magic. However, this was the first time I'd seen him since David's funeral.

Before Foggy walked in the door, no one was in the shop except for me. I was watching a new YouTube video on the store's computer by the cash register. It was a video essay about why it's hard to make a good third movie in a trilogy. I watch a lot of YouTube at the shop, but I was quite entranced by this one. Nonetheless, as soon as I saw Foggy, I completely lost focus on the video. I didn't pause it or turn it off though. I just let it continue to play in the background.

"Welcome to Galaxy's Comics and Games," I said as the door opened. "Oh, hi, Foggy!" I said after seeing who it was. I was trying not to sound too perky. I knew he was grieving like I was, and I wanted to be sensitive. He had a grim and serious look on his face.

Foggy walked up to the counter. He stared at me without smiling or saying a word. I felt like he wasn't blinking.

"I got a new binder of Magic singles in," I said, breaking the awkward silence. "Someone sold me their entire collection the other day. You want to see it?"

This new binder of Magic: The Gathering cards wasn't displayed yet. I was keeping it behind the counter until I flipped through it. I did this just in case there was anything super valuable in the binder that should be kept in a safer location. However, I trust Foggy to flip through the new binder for me. And this isn't the first time I've let him do this. This is how he's been able to get first dibs on rare cards before I even knew they were in the store.

"Not really. Honestly, there were always better shops to buy Magic singles at. Not that I haven't found some gems here before, but mostly, I was just hanging out with friends," Foggy said.

"Ahh..." I said. "Well, let me know if you need any help with anything."

"Don't give me that generic, retail worker shit. David was a crazy-ass dude, but he's been my best friend since Junior High. And I want to know who killed him," Foggy said.

A chill went up my spine. It felt like the hair on my arms stood up. Of course, Foggy wants to know the killer's identity. I do too. However, unless I missed some implied, neurotypical nonsense, this was the first time I'd heard anyone wonder about it out loud.

It felt like Foggy had just blurted out something that other people had probably been thinking but were not saying. Maybe they feared that violence could happen to them next. Maybe they were unwilling to talk about a hard subject that was tough to think about. Or maybe they were simply waiting for the police investigation to play out before making wild speculations or accusations. But regardless of why no one else was talking about this, I agreed with Foggy that it should be discussed.

"You know, I wonder about that myself," I said. "It was weird. It was as if the killer targeted David. It didn't feel random at all. I know they killed James, Brian and Robert, but it kind of felt like my shop was the other target."

Foggy nodded.

"The killer was using a voice modulator to sound like Ghostface from the *Scream* movies. And it sounded like they were a part of ComicsGate. Like, they said something about how this rampage was for 'woke' agendas ruining comics or something," I continued.

Foggy's expression warmed. It also looked like he was deep in thought.

"You know, I think I'll look through that new Magic binder after all, Eric," Foggy said.

I smiled and said, "No probs. If you see anything valuable in there, let me know. I haven't even gone through it yet." I pulled out the binder of MTG cards from behind the counter and handed it to him.

For about 15 minutes, Foggy flipped through the binder in complete silence. When it became obvious that he wasn't saying anything, I went back to focusing on the YouTube video that was still playing.

"I think it was someone who's lurked inside the walls of this comic shop," Foggy said, startling me and pulling my focus back to him. 'I suspected this before but now I just know it. It's got to be someone we know, dude. The news article that quoted you didn't even mention that the killer was, like, a toxic fan or a ComicsGater."

I paused the YouTube video.

"Honestly, I might've left out that part when talking to the reporter. These past few weeks have felt like a blur," I said.

"Yeah, they have. I wish I were there when it happened," Foggy said.

"What do you mean?" I asked.

"Me and David have been there for each other in every chapter of our lives. He's helped me through breakups. I celebrated with him when he graduated from law school. Maybe if I had been there when he died, I could've stopped it," Foggy said.

"I have survivor's guilt too. I've lost so much sleep because of it. But Foggy, I don't think you being here would've changed anything. David was my friend too, you know. But the guy had a chainsaw. You couldn't have stopped that," I said.

"Look, I appreciate your concern, but you're not my fucking therapist," Foggy replied. "I just want to know who killed my friend."

"Yeah, I hear you," I said.

Foggy closed the binder of Magic cards. He was starting to look deep in thought again.

"Who in the store has weird views like that? Who has gotten into an argument with David before? I mean, a real fucking argument – not, like, two nerds bonding," Foggy said.

I knew this question was rhetorical. Because Foggy and David were mostly in here at the same time. It wasn't like David was getting into heated debates at Galaxy's without Foggy's presence. Or at the very least, if he did, I was sure Foggy would've heard about it.

"I feel like David's probably rubbed a few people the wrong way over the years," I said.

"Yeah, well, I don't remember anyone like that guy Adrian," Foggy said.

I started to feel dizzy. My tongue was feeling larger and heavier. Was I forgetting something? Was it something about the night the killer was here? I don't remember much about that night. But was I blocking out something direly important?

Stop it. Hold yourself together, Eric.

I stopped and took three deep breaths. My eyes were closed as I did this. I finally spoke after opening them back up.

"Yeah," I said. "Of course, I remember Adrian."

Chapter 12

Adrian was a regular customer for years. He wasn't someone who often expressed his opinions in the shop, like David or even Blake. This wasn't really a hangout spot for him like it is for many regular customers. Adrian mostly just came to the shop, bought his comic books and left. He didn't typically talk to me or anyone else about what he was reading unless he was making a change to his subscriptions. Only occasionally did he even browse the shop.

Foggy is usually a quiet guy, but quiet like a wallflower not a ghost. Compared to Adrian, Foggy is more talkative than a character in an Aaron Sorkin flick. There's a chance that part of why Adrian was so quiet was because he felt like he was unable to truly express himself at Galaxy's Comics & Games. However, before the incident that happened the last time he was here, this never occurred to me. I just thought that he wasn't the talkative type – at least not at the comic shop.

A few years back, Adrian was picking up his subscriptions. Before paying, he browsed the new books on the shelf. At the time, *Captain Marvel* was playing in movie theaters. While browsing, he overheard me and David talking about *Captain Marvel*, the online outrage surrounding the movie and the Marvel Cinematic Universe in general. David was being loud and opinionated as usual. Before Adrian spoke up, I believe David used the term "man-babies" to describe many of those who were complaining about *Captain Marvel* and the movie's star, Brie Larson. I suspect that Adrian was irritated and felt the need to speak up for his own viewpoint.

After Adrian walked back to the cash register, he said Brie Larson had alienated "the fans" with her comments about not liking "white dudes." David said that's not what she said. Larson was saying there wasn't enough representation among film critics. The statement that got her in hot water was "I don't want to hear what a white man has to say about *A Wrinkle in Time*. I want to hear what a woman of color, a biracial woman, has to say." The context was that *A Wrinkle in Time* was a movie from a Black female director with a biracial, Black, female lead. And it was panned by critics (who are predominantly white and male.)

Adrian doubled down and said, "Whatever she said, she was basically telling white male fans not to watch the movie." He said Disney was lying about *Captain Marvel*'s box office numbers because they were covering for Brie Larson's PR disaster. He said *Captain Marvel* wasn't a box office success like it was reported to be. He said the "fake news media" was lying too. He claimed that his friend saw *Captain Marvel* in theaters and the auditorium was empty.

After hearing this, David asked Adrian, "Don't movie theater chains report the ticket sales – not Disney"? There was a long pause. I don't think Adrian knew what to say. Breaking the silence, David made fun of him. He said, "You're more delusional than Mad Hatter ranting in Arkham."

I couldn't help but chuckle at David's analogy. I was trying not to laugh. So, the sound that escaped me couldn't have been too loud. Perhaps it wasn't a chuckle but a snicker. But whatever it was, as soon as Adrian heard me laugh, he exploded. Up until that moment, he'd been mostly speaking in a calm tone of voice, but not anymore.

He loudly and furiously said, "You SJW freaks are the delusional ones – not me." I'm not sure if he knew or not that me and David were autistic, but he then yelled, "Those of us in the silent majority are sick and tired of your retarded, liberal bullshit!" He stormed out of the comic shop without saying goodbye. He didn't even buy the comic books he had with him at the cash register. He never returned to Galaxy's Comics & Games again. From the store's phone, I called him a couple times to "remind" him about his pull list, but he didn't pick up. The last I heard from him was a Facebook message that simply read, "I should've known better than to trust an SJW." As far as I know, no one else heard from him ever again.

Before this day, I only vaguely knew that Adrian was right-wing. Except for perhaps the use of the "r-word" the last time he was here, I never heard him say anything overtly bigoted. I certainly never perceived him to be saying or doing anything that could make others feel unwelcome at Galaxy's.

Ironically, I think it was David who made him feel emboldened to start rattling off this deranged conspiracy theory. David has that way with people at the comic shop – getting them to open up and share their thoughts and feelings. Except, in my experience, he usually has this way with likeminded people. But also, like Adrian, David was a 30-something year old white man. I think Adrian felt more comfortable speaking freely than he otherwise may have.

David later told me that he made the joke comparing Adrian to a Batman villain because he'd "lost his cool." In other words, while he may have said it in a somewhat playful tone, it was coming from a place of anger. David said he was thinking about all the online harassment that Brie Larson was experiencing at the time. David suspected that Adrian was one of the trolls harassing her. David expressed remorse, saying that he should've handled that situation differently.

In my opinion, David's suspicion had a lot of merit. The conspiracy theory that Adrian espoused sounded like something that only someone who follows the worst people on the internet would ever believe. If he supported online harassment campaigns such as ComicsGate or the so-called "Fandom Menace," he never really expressed it in the shop, but he probably did online.

Adrian lived close by, and I don't think he wanted to travel further away to buy his comics. But I guess he was too angry and/or embarrassed to ever return to Galaxy's. Honestly, I can't help but wonder if the real reason why he never came back was because he just didn't have the courage to express his views again. I suspect he didn't want to see me or David without sticking up for his culturally conservative perspective. But at the same time, he knew that if he did see either of us again, he'd chicken out. Maybe Adrian predicted that I was about to start laying down ground rules like a Discord moderator – and say something like, "Please don't use the R-word in my shop ever again." Maybe he went home and felt like I, Mr. Joseph Stalin, was going to start telling him what to do. But I guess we'll never really know what was going through his head.

It sucked to lose a regular customer. Comic shops and other small businesses don't operate with large profit margins. Everyone with a pull list can make a difference in my livelihood. Also, it sucked because Adrian left about 50 dollars' worth of comics that I'd special ordered for him. I waited two months before I stopped ordering copies for his subscription box. When it was clear that he wasn't coming back, I emptied his box and put the comic books on the shelf. A few of them were never sold and eventually moved into the back issue boxes. Today's Adrian's pull list box has someone else's name on it.

Blake thought it was hilarious when David told him what happened. He said he thought it was great that "someone called him out on his bullshit." In this conversation, David told Blake that he really admired how much he could keep his cool in the face of what he described as "bigots and trolls." It ended up being an ironic back-and-forth where they both told each other "You're the man" but for opposite reasons.

When Blake told Anna about the incident, she wasn't amused like he was. Blake presented it as a funny story, but she wasn't smiling or laughing. She said it's too bad that Galaxy's Comics & Games lost a "good customer" but "it is what it is." However, at the same time, Anna admitted that she never liked Adrian. She even went as far as to describe him as "creepy." This led me to believe that something about Adrian may have been in my blind spot. I asked Anna what she meant but she didn't elaborate. She just said, "Never mind. Don't worry about it."

As for Foggy – well, he was just a few feet away from David and Adrian when the incident occurred. He was flipping through a binder of Magic: The Gathering singles like he always was. But even if he was there, I don't think I'd ever even heard him speak Adrian's name until today.

Chapter 13

"Are you saying you think Adrian may have killed David and the others?" I asked.

"I don't know. He certainly had a motive. He snapped once so maybe he snapped again," Foggy said.

I thought about this for a moment.

"He didn't really snap that day, though," I said.

"Man, I might not have gotten involved, but I was right there when it happened. Adrian was ranting about some bullshit he probably heard from a really bad YouTube video. It sounded like he was of those hashtag 'gate' assholes that David hated," Foggy said.

"I don't care for them either," I said.

"Me either. But you know what I mean," Foggy said. "David had Twitter and Instagram followers specifically because he was into all that political shit."

"Right. And what happened with Adrian that day kind of felt like an argument that would usually be online. But it happened in 'real life' here. When I heard Adrian saying that stuff, I didn't want to argue. But David made fun of him and called him delusional," I said.

"Exactly. And maybe now he wants payback. He seems like the type," Foggy said.

"Really? The type to brutally murder people? Honestly, before that day, I don't think I ever even had a negative thought about Adrian. And if he does want revenge, why now? Why wait until years later?" I asked.

"I don't fucking know. But someone did this shit, and I want justice for my friend," Foggy said.

Is Foggy talking about vigilantism? I know we're in a comic shop and there are many stories glorifying the idea. But this is real life, not a comic book.

"I don't know what we can do," I proclaimed. "Maybe we could talk to the police and–"

"Fuck the police," Foggy interrupted. "They won't take this seriously. Cops don't understand nerd shit."

I can't say I trust the police either, especially with all the viral Black Lives Matter videos I've seen. But I didn't really know what Foggy meant.

"I guess," I said.

"It's like, when I was in high school, someone stole my binder of all my rare Magic cards. I reported it to the police, and they didn't do shit. They didn't understand that I was talking about thousands of dollars' worth of property that took me years to collect. They looked at me like I was an idiot. The cops filled out some bullshit paperwork to shut me up and never 'investigated' anything," Foggy said.

"That's not the same thing as a murder case though," I said.

"Yes, it is. I almost never check Twitter. But even I know that you should probably keep your distance from those 'SJWs are ruining comics' guys. It's suspicious. But normies don't get how it's suspicious, and cops are fucking normies," Foggy said. I nodded. I think I understood what he meant.

"You said when the killer was here, he was rambling about

woke agendas or whatever. That sure sounds like Adrian. And he had a motive to kill David especially," Foggy said.

"Yeah, you already said that. I just don't want to accuse someone of a serious crime without a shred of evidence. I don't even know what we can do about this other than going to the police," I said.

Foggy nodded, seeming to agree. There was a short pause before I spoke again.

"If Adrian is the killer, why didn't he kill me? I think he was just as mad at me as he was at David," I said.
Foggy laughed. This was the first time I'd seen him smile since the massacre.

"Yeah, no, he wasn't," Foggy said.

"Maybe not. But that still doesn't change the question," I said.

There was another short pause before Foggy replied.

"I don't know why. And look, I know we're not in a Batman or Punisher movie. So, maybe you're right. Maybe we should go to the police tonight and tell them what we know. They can laugh at me again. But at least we'll be doing what we can," Foggy said.

I didn't know what to say. Maybe we should simply let the police conduct their investigation – and answer any questions about the massacre they may have. Going to the police to accuse someone, even vaguely, seems like a bad idea. Nonetheless, I understood Foggy's viewpoint and why he feels the way he does. I wanted justice for David, Brian, Robert and James too.

"Do what you think is best," I said. "I trust you to handle this. And if the police have any further questions, I can answer them."

Foggy nodded.

"Thanks, Eric. Good talk," Foggy said with a smile. He tapped the Magic the Gathering binder and said, "I didn't see anything super rare in here. But I didn't finish looking through it either."

"Sounds good," I said. "I can look through the rest."

"I'm not buying anything today, but I'll see ya later," Foggy said.

"You too," I said to Foggy as he walked out the door of Galaxy's Comics & Games.

I turned the YouTube video back on. But a few minutes later, I heard it. It was the same sound that I heard in my dreams every night. It was the sound I heard the night David, James, Brian and Robert were killed. Could it be? Am I really hearing a chainsaw again?

I ran outside. As soon as I exited the shop, I no longer heard it. However, my feeling of panic remained. I looked around in all directions. Did something happen to Foggy too?

Following where I heard the sound coming from, I ran to the parking lot across the street. It was here where my sneaking suspicion turned into a terrifying reality.

All the doors of Foggy's car were still closed. The driver's side door and window were covered in blood. My eyes locked with the wet, red splashes as I scanned the top of the window to the bottom of the door. Lying on the ground in front of the door, Foggy was a bloody mess. He wasn't moving.

Everything started to spin. I was losing my balance until I noticed something else. There was a note on the windshield under the wiper blades. It looked like a flier someone left for the driver to see – or like a note someone might leave after a fender bender.

I walked around to the front of the car. I knew it was a crime scene, but I had to read it. Against my better judgment, I grabbed the note off the car's windshield. I read it.

"To whom this may concern,

It had to be done. There was no other way. I had to stop this beta male.

Like a woke comic book canceled by the publisher in the middle of an arc, the SJWs must die.

Sincerely yours,

The #ComicsGate Killer"

Chapter 14

I sat at home watching television in the basement. The images flashed back at me, but I wasn't paying attention. I couldn't focus on anything. I'd become a prisoner in my own head with conflicting thoughts and feelings battling for dominance.

It had been a week since Foggy was killed outside of Galaxy's Comics & Games. This time the inside of the shop wasn't considered to be the crime scene. So, there was no police tape or police order to keep the store closed. And yet that's exactly what I was doing.

Even if the violence didn't happen inside of my store, I was still the survivor who found the body. I was still the one who dialed 911. When the police questioned me, they wrote down everything as I talked. I told them about Adrian. I told them how minutes before Foggy was killed, he was talking to me about going to go to the police. I told them how Foggy suspected Adrian of killing the others. I told them about ComicsGate, their anger about so-called "woke" comic books and what the note left at the crime scene was clearly alluding to.

But it didn't seem like they were listening to anything I said. The police looked annoyed and acted like I was on an irrelevant tangent. I was an autistic nerd on a silly rant. It sounded like they viewed the location of the murders, the parking lot outside of my comic shop, as just a coincidence. They asked if David and Foggy had any enemies outside of Galaxy's that I knew about. I guess they did ask about the killer's note because they asked me what a "beta male" was. They didn't seem to accept my answer, though. I told them it's just an insult that right-wing, culture war trolls say online. One of the officers asked, "Are you sure the note didn't mean something else? How close did you say David and Foggy were?"

The ordeal had an eerie similarity to how Foggy described the police responding to him when an unknown thief stole his rare Magic cards. After talking to the police, I put up a sign on the front door of Galaxy's that simply said: "We are temporarily closed until further notice."

Customers knew that another Galaxy's regular had been killed. The local news article about Foggy's murder didn't mention this detail, but word travels fast. This past week, I'd been receiving Facebook messages and texts asking what was going on and when or if Galaxy's was reopening. Comic book fans were calling the shop about their pull lists, wondering if they should start going to a new shop. Gamers wanted to know if Friday Night Magic at Galaxy's was going to become history. But even after a week of saying nothing, I still didn't know what to say to anyone. I was still trying to figure out what to do next.

Long before the murders began, if I didn't personally know a customer at the shop, I often found myself side eyeing them. If a customer said the wrong thing, I wondered if they were part of an online harassment campaign such as ComicsGate. For instance, if a customer said, "I hate how political comic books have become," my guard immediately went up. Complaining about "politics" in comic books has become code for complaining about the increasing representation of women, people of color and/or LGBT people. Tensing up wasn't always my response to statements like this. There was a time when I gave my fellow comic book fans the benefit of doubt. It felt like so long ago. Because toxic fans changed everything.

Perhaps I'd been naïve in the past. Perhaps that's what statements like that, in the context of entertainment media, always meant. But toxic fans took the gloves off – or at least they did online. They exposed something that had always been bubbling underneath the surface among toxic men and bigoted, reactionary, exclusionary fans.

These toxic fans brutally harassed prominent progressives, especially women, in nerd culture. When gathering others to join in on the harassment, they used slogans and hashtags that you had to be in the know to recognize the meaning behind. Comic book readers were in the know. Star Wars fans were in the know. Video games enthusiasts were in the know. We recognized what these dog whistles meant. For those of us disgusted by the behavior, it felt like they were using our own fandoms against us. They used images of galactic empires, cartoon frogs and *Green Lantern* comic book villains that we recognized. We watched in horror as these beloved, recognizable images were used to preach and promote hate. But the "normies"? The "squares"? "The "jocks"? Or whatever it is you want to call "the people who don't understand nerds"? They didn't get it. These fascist memes and sexist hashtags went over their heads. When we tried to explain it to them, we appeared just as strange and hysterical as those committing the harassment.

A lot of the time when those facing online harassment turned to their male, straight, cisgender or white colleagues who they trusted, it was radio silence. Colleagues didn't speak out on social media or in interviews. I've been told they offered support behind the scenes. But they didn't publicly – never publicly. This is when men with attitudes like David and Blake felt the need to step in. They began screaming every day to their 200 Twitter followers about how much these sexist creeps, these man-babies, these racist pieces of garbage, really sucked. "You're a white knight" and "you're a beta male" the harassers screamed back at them. It was pure nerd rage. Only it was now coming from two sides instead of one.

A so-called "left-wing" side of the nerdy culture war emerged. But remember, this culture war was started by people who were mad about seeing more representation of women, LGBT people and people of color in nerd culture and media. Before getting involved, these left-wing, comic book guys' tweets were mostly positive statements about comic books, movies, and video games. Afterwards, they were getting unfollowed more and more by people who told them to "shut up about politics." But simultaneously, their overall follower counts more than doubled. They gained a social media audience of others who were against the harassment campaigns.

But like Batman and the Joker, both sides needed each other. If you stopped talking about the harassment campaigns, you'd lose engagement. You'd lost followers. The algorithm won't show your posts on feeds as often. It'll be harder to promote your podcast. You might not get enough backers for your next Kickstarter campaign to be successful. When you plug the artwork you have for sale, potential buyers won't see it. In short, you'll fail in your creative endeavors. Because you'll lose your audience. After all, they didn't follow you to hear how much you enjoyed *Captain Marvel*, *The Last Jedi*, or the 2016 *Ghostbusters* film. They followed you so you could scream at the guy who said Brie Larson wasn't smiling enough on the movie posters. Unless it's presidential campaign season, these followers don't even want you posting about actual politics. They just want you reacting to the culture war reactionaries.

Fox News, to better compete with right-wing YouTube channels and podcasts, started talking non-stop about "cancel culture" and the "woke mobs." They told their audience that leftist "thugs" online were "canceling" those who either voiced support for online harassment or actively encouraged it. Donald Trump, as a 2016 presidential candidate, whined on camera about how they're making the Ghostbusters women, pandering to toxic fans everywhere. Ted Cruz, an actual United States Senator, quote tweeted toxic fans with laugh reacts and smile emojis. Bill Maher, a so-called "moderate liberal," echoed Fox News on his late-night talk show. Maher even invited a prominent GamerGater onto his show to laugh and shoot the breeze. But in all this dishonest framing, these comedians, pundits and politicians either conveniently left out the part about online harassment, downplayed it or outright lied about it.

To many, when these women in nerd culture complained about what they were experiencing, they were thought to be crying wolf. They were thought to be attention-seeking liars. In fact, to normies and conservatives alike, it was believed to be the exact opposite situation that it was. They bought into the idea that public figures facing online harassment were directing a so-called "woke mob" of supporters. While there was sometimes a nugget of truth to this framing, it was reversing the cause and effect.

But let's never forget about the other key players in all of this – Mark Zuckerberg, Jack Dorsey, Elon Musk – those who own or have owned the social media companies. Whether it's positive or negative, they've made a lot of money on any kind of engagement. Don't forget about Rupert Murdoch, the owner of Fox News. Let's certainly not forget about Jeffrey Bewkes, the CEO of Warner Corporation, who pays Bill Maher more than the left-wing, Emmy-award-winning, late-night talk show host John Oliver. Maybe write down the names of those rich guys on a list. Because they're much more important than whatever YouTuber or podcaster you're replying to on Twitter.

Amidst all of this, another position in the nerdy culture war emerged. Awareness of this vicious, never-ending cycle caused some of us to say, "don't talk about ComicsGate," "don't talk about GamerGate" or "don't talk about the Fandom Menace." After all, saying the name of the harassment campaign only draws attention to it. These true centrists said, "don't feed the trolls." I describe us as "true" centrists because we're not like those who dismissed the harassment as not being real. We never said "both sides are bad" when one was engaging in harassment and the other was reacting to it. Also, we're not colleagues who really should've publicly supported those being harassed from the start. We're just fans who don't want to add to this vicious cycle.

That's the attitude that me and Foggy always had about all of this – a fat lot of good it did him, though.

As the TV blared, I pulled my phone out of my pocket. Anna was there for me after David was killed. I thought she'd be a good person to confide in again. But I didn't know what to say. I sat and stared at my phone for who knows how long. Finally, I started typing.

I sent her a text that said, "Did I ever tell you about the guy on Twitter who told me to kill myself for liking *The Last Jedi*?"

I stared at my phone's screen. It turned from Sent to Read. I then saw she was typing a response.

"IDK. Maybe? Doesn't sound like a unique story. Star Wars fans were pissed about that one. I bet Rian Johnson and Kelly Marie Tran were getting messages like that every day," she said.

I wrote back, "Yeah, but I don't really get into it with people online. I know a woman or POC is more likely to receive harassment. David liked to argue with people, so he developed thick skin too. But this was literally just some rando telling me to kill myself. Because I tweeted that I liked the movie."

Anna read it. She didn't reply. I kept waiting for her to say something, but she didn't. Finally, I sent her another text.

"Sorry if this doesn't sound like a big deal. But it's on my mind with everything else going on," I said.

The text turned from Sent to Read. This time I could see Anna replying.

"I'm sorry, man. Trolls suck. You know I deleted my social media because of harassment," Anna said.

"Yeah," I replied.

"You gonna reopen the store?" Anna asked.

I stared at the text message. I didn't know what to say, not even to Anna. But I felt like I had to say something.

"We'll see," I replied before putting my phone back in my pocket.

I heard a reply, but I ignored it. I was once again trying to focus on the television and not think about any of this – as if, even before the murders by this so-called "ComicsGate Killer," that was possible.

Chapter 15

I once ate a bad chicken parmesan sandwich and threw up all night. The sandwich's toxicity temporarily harmed me, but I made a full recovery in just a day. However, so-called "toxic" fans aren't like spoiled chicken or rotten cheese. They're poisonous like a scorpion's tail or the bite of a brown recluse spider. They poison our joyful thoughts and our feelings of safety. Their poison can consume everything in a fandom if it goes unchecked. They kill the warmth for each other that we once felt. These poisonous fans kill our communities. They ruin places that we once loved. Even something as sacred as the comic shop can lose itself as a place of refuge.

And now there appears to be a poisonous fan that isn't just metaphorically killing fandom but literally killing it. A poisonous fan has been killing off the regular customers at Galaxy's Comics & Games. I wish it were as easy as pinning these crimes on Adrian. I know Foggy strongly suspected him, but I just don't know.

In the comic book *Death of Elvira*, Elvira's Twitter trolls are described as "armchair basement dwellers hangry at mom for being slow with the Hot Pockets." The horror television host is killed by an anonymous nutjob mailing her an explosive. This is after receiving a death threat from a poisonous fan online.

Death of Elvira was published at a time when many millennials still lived with their parents. This is because of the rising costs of housing and a shrinking number of opportunities for entry-level positions after college. The stereotype of trolls being so-called "basement dwellers" has some implications. It implies that an individual who makes enough money to afford rent or home ownership wouldn't harass a celebrity online – or at least would be less likely to do it. It can't be homeowning, baby boomer men tweeting hateful, sexist garbage at Elvira, Brie Larson or female comic book creators and game developers. It's "basement dwellers," right? The anonymous troll couldn't possibly be old, cranky and prosperous. Poisonous fans must be young, broke and entitled… right?

Well, to quote a popular GIF, "I don't know about that one, chief." Poisonous fans make multi-hundred-dollar donations to "ComicsGate" Indiegogo campaigns to "own" or "trigger" the libs. Angry Star Wars fans raised millions of dollars in a Go-FundMe to pressure Disney to re-shoot *The Last Jedi*. Poisonous fans often pine for how pop culture and comic books supposedly used to be so much better in the 1980s and 1990s. They think everything new is bad because of so-called "forced diversity." Meanwhile, in those good old days, most people in their 20s and 30s were either children or not even born yet.

So, why are millennials who still live with their parents so often the punching bag when a person is mad about anonymous trolls? At the end of the day, a poisonous fan can be anyone. An anonymous troll can be anyone. A masked killer can be anyone. That's what makes them so terrifying.

This so-called "ComicsGate killer" might be Adrian or they might be someone else. It would give me such peace of mind if I knew the identity of this deranged psychopath. But I don't. I know Foggy blamed Adrian. But there's no way Adrian was the only ComicsGater to ever walk through the door of Galaxy's Comics & Games. There are many strangers who could potentially hold those views and support that harassment campaign, but I wouldn't even know it.

I continued to watch television while I pet my cat Stretch sitting on my lap. My brother Marshal played *Final Fantasy XIV* on the computer nearby, occasionally taking hits off his THC vape pen.

Marshal is a 7th grade History teacher. Both my parents have what you might call "middle-class" incomes. My brother and I live with them.

My father had the day off. My mom and brother worked today but he got home a little earlier than she did. After my mother got home, she came down to the basement to say hello to me and my brother. It wasn't until hours later that I walked upstairs to the living room to talk to her and Dad.

My parents were sitting on the couch. My mom was reading a book. My dad was nursing a beer as he watched *Thursday Night Football*.

I decided it was time to spit it out. I had to tell them what was on my mind.

"I don't think reopening the store is safe for me or my customers – certainly not until the police catch the killer. But I don't know if they ever will," I said.

My parents exchanged worried looks. My mother reached over and grabbed the bookmark that was on the table in front of her. She put the bookmark in her book and set it down in the same place.

"Why do you say that?" my mother asked.

"Well, you got to understand that this guy is calling himself 'the ComicsGate killer.' ComicsGate is a hashtag movement about opposing so-called 'forced diversity' and progressive politics in comics," I said. "ComicsGaters might not have killed before, as far as I know, but their whole M.O. is being relentless. They harassed —"

"Look, I'm gonna stop you right there, Eric," my father interrupted. "What does this have to do with closing down the shop? That's your entire source of income."

I stared at him. I was stunned and didn't know what to say. "Honey, I think what Eric is trying to say is that the killer is still on the loose and is likely to target his store again," my mom said.

"Yeah," I said. "I don't know why this killer is specifically targeting my shop or my customers. But the note that was left by Foggy's dead body was very clear about their agenda."

"And what agenda is that?" my father asked.

"I – I – just told you," I stammered.

My mom gave a worried glance at my father again, but he continued to stare at me.

"Dad, whoever is doing this can't just be killing randomly. They're targeting people in the name of their hashtag movement," I said.

"Even if you're right, I don't give a damn. Terrorists say a lot of things," my dad said. "You can't cut off your only source of income. What are you going to do? Go back to barely making minimum wage at the library? Cut it out, Eric. You need that store. And that's the bottom line."

When I was in college, I worked at the local library as a page. Meaning, a few days a week, I stacked books and put them away. After graduation, I continued to work this job part time. My major was Journalism & Media Studies, and my minor was Computer Science. But even after years of searching, I never found work in either of my fields.

When my cousin Jeremy bought Galaxy's Comics & Games from its previous owner, he asked me to help run the shop. He didn't know a lot about comics, but he loved Magic: The Gathering and other games. When Jeremy co-owned the shop, he was mostly only there on Friday nights and during the day on Saturdays and Sundays. In addition to his paralegal day job, he helped with organizing the store and running the Friday Night Magic tournaments. Also, Jeremy was generally the face of Galaxy's when we spoke to the press or in any kind of Public Relations capacity. This arrangement worked well because I didn't know as much about games as Jeremy did. And he didn't suffer from social anxiety like I do.

After a few years of this arrangement, Jeremy proposed to his fiancé, and everything changed. He moved further away to a more "family friendly" suburban area with less hustle and bustle. Jeremy had other responsibilities now. He had a lot on his plate, and he had to drop some of it. His office day job was enough. So, he sold his half of the store to me. Since then, I've been the sole owner of Galaxy's Comics & Games.

To fill Jeremy's void, my parents help out at the store. My father is the store's accountant. He helped build shelving units for the back issue boxes too. My mother runs the cash register when I'm unavailable. Both help with customer service on Free Comic Book Day, Halloween ComicFest and during our Black Friday sale on back issues.

"I have skills," I proclaimed.

"What skills? Newspapers? Broadcasting? Ones and zeros?" my dad said.

Not this again. How is that even sarcasm? He's just stating

facts.

"Yeah," I said. "Those are marketable skills."

"Eric, the news industry is dying," my mom said, chiming in. "There aren't a lot of journalism jobs, especially for someone whose only experience is working for a college newspaper ten years ago."

"Exactly. Listen to your mother," my dad said. "Besides, when shit hits the fan, I don't want my own son with the fake news media. You're a good businessman selling funny books. I don't want you to become an enemy of the American people."

I rolled my eyes. But I couldn't get into it with him about this. I had to focus on what mattered right now.

"But also, like you said, I know how to code," I proclaimed. My father took another sip of his beer. My mother looked at him and then at me.

"Maybe a new career path would be good for you," she said. "But you shouldn't ever quit a job without a clear idea of what you're doing next. If you're worried about your safety at the store, maybe we can hire security."

"I can't afford to hire a security guard. I can't even afford a cashier. As it is, Galaxy's barely even scrapes by," I said.

There was a long pause in the conversation before my father spoke again.

"How about this? I'll hire a security guard for a month. This'll be out of my own pocket. We can think of it as an investment. Because the store needs to stay open. It's your only source of income," my dad said.

"What about after the month is over?" I asked.

"Well," my dad said. He took another sip of beer and continued, "we can deal with that then. But I'm assuming you won't need a security guard forever – only until all this blows over."

He doesn't get it. He just doesn't get it. Neither of them do.

"I don't know if this will ever blow over. That's what I'm trying to tell you," I said.

"Eric, enough!" my dad said, slamming down his beer bottle.

"It was probably a hate crime," my dad declared. "And that's horrible – but it has nothing to do with you or your store. Weren't David and Foggy gay?"

"What? No, they weren't gay. What are you talking about?" I asked.

"So, they were just two single men in their thirties who were joined at the hip? They sound like faggots to me," my dad said.

My fists clenched and my teeth grinded together. I wasn't going to hit my father. It was just a reflex. I knew he'd been drinking. I took a deep breath before replying so I wouldn't say something I might regret.

"Dad, don't say things like that to me. You know I have LGBT friends and customers. But no, David and Foggy were straight," I said.

"Even if they weren't actually gay, I still think it was a hate crime. This deranged lunatic probably thought they were gay. Are you really expecting a deranged lunatic to double check?" my father said.

"Maybe," I replied.

"I know in college, they taught you 'it's all about society. It's society, man,'" my dad said, with a voice imitating Cheech and Chong. "But the real world doesn't always line up with that snowflake bullshit. This guy was sick. He was fucked up in the head and that's that. Hate crime or not, that's all I need to know about this freak," my dad said.

"What's your point, Dad?" I said, getting even more irritated.

"My point is that he's not after you, your customers or your shop, Eric! He's just a nutcase. It's not that we have nothing to worry about. But this killer is something that me, your mother and everyone else in the neighborhood has to worry about too."

"He'll get what's coming to him in hell," my mom said, chiming in.

"Yes, he will. Yes, he will," my dad said, nodding before taking another sip of his beer.

Chapter 16

I reopened Galaxy's Comics & Games the following Tuesday. I spent Monday organizing the new books that came in last week while the shop was closed. On Tuesday, this week's new books came in too. I kept myself busy organizing them as well.

Unfortunately, it was becoming harder to focus on the YouTube videos and artists' livestreams I played at the shop to keep myself happy and entertained. What was once a great escape was turning into background noise. Instead of enjoying them, I buried myself in the task of organizing and reorganizing the store.

Maybe my father is right. Maybe this so-called "ComicsGate killer" isn't really a ComicsGate killer after all. Maybe they're just a nutcase. Who knows?

Whatever motivated the murders, I had to stop thinking about it. I pushed away my fearful thoughts and dreadful feelings. If I ever tensed up, I reminded myself that a security guard was present now. He always stood silently in front of the wall of new books. Whenever I looked his way, he appeared alert, and it comforted me.

I began calling other comic shops, asking if I could sell all my back issues to them at wholesale prices. If I were to find myself unemployed and looking for other work, the money could possibly keep me afloat. If I were to start doing something else with my life, Galaxy's could be sold to another owner. Or I could just find ways to sell all the products inside the shop and let someone else have the store space. I wasn't planning on permanently closing Galaxy's, but it doesn't hurt to investigate these things, right?

It's too bad David wasn't here anymore. He knew all about selling comic books online. If he were still alive, he'd be able to help me with that. But I couldn't think about my dead friends without breaking down. And I must stand tall. I need to be able to remain a functional human being, especially in public.

I'm so conflicted, but I couldn't think about it. I couldn't think about any of it. I had to just continue my routine to the best of my ability.

I hadn't seen Blake or Anna since the night before Foggy was killed. I hadn't heard from Blake since then either. He wasn't one of the customers calling, texting or Facebook messaging, asking me if or when the shop was reopening. Many of Blake's Yu-Gi-Oh buddies continued to hang out at the gaming tables, but not him.

It was late in the afternoon on a Thursday. Before Blake walked in the door, no one was inside the shop except for me and the security guard. I'm guessing Blake recently ended his morning shift at the restaurant. Because he had something personal to tell me, I suspect he was stopping by on Thursday instead of Wednesday to avoid the presence of too many other customers. I didn't even say "hi, welcome to Galaxy's Comics and Games" because I immediately noticed it was him.

"Hey, Blake," I said.

"Hey, Eric. What's up?" he said.

Of all the regulars at the comic shop, Blake has probably

been the most outgoing. He's always talking to both the gamers in the back of the store and the Wednesday warriors buying comic books. However, Blake wasn't his usual perky, upbeat, positive self today. He looked sad, somber and a little droopy.

"Nothing much. Just been getting some stuff done. The back issues desperately needed to be reorganized," I said.

"That's cool," Blake said. "Hey, I didn't want to ghost ya. I wanted to tell you face to face about what's going on with me."

"Okay," I said.

"Galaxy's has been like a home away from home and my favorite place to socialize. But I don't think I can come here anymore," Blake said. "I mean, maybe I'll be back here someday. But I'm thinking I'm gonna lay low for now – and I will for a long time."

"I understand. But what about how we shouldn't let the terrorists win?" I asked.

"That was after one incident. This is a full-on killing spree now. A masked maniac could be back here any day," Blake said.

I said nothing. What could I say? Despite what my dad said, Blake was right. Even with hired security, I didn't know if my customers and I were safe. Maybe I should "lay low" too – meaning, close down or sell the shop.

"I'm sorry, Eric. You got my number if you ever want to chill," Blake said.

I nodded.

"And look, man, honestly, it's not just about the violence. I used to be able to come here and almost breathe a sigh of relief. This shop was a safe place and now it's not. Galaxy's will never be what it once meant to me," Blake said.

I felt that. He was right. It'll never be the same for me either.

And I'm the one who's supposed to be running this store.

"Makes sense," I said.

Blake stared at me, like he was hoping I'd say more. I didn't, though. I didn't know what to say. Instead, I asked him about something else that was eating away at me.

"Who do you think did it? Who do you think killed them?" I asked.

Blake shook his head.

"I don't know, and I don't care. It's not relevant. This place is forever tainted. Our friends are never coming back," Blake said.

I nodded and said, "They aren't." I may have been getting a little choked up.

"Eric, I know we live in a society where men aren't supposed to talk about our feelings. But this shit can eat away at you, man. We need to look out for each other," Blake said.

It's not just about expressing feelings. I didn't even know how I felt but I knew I was doubting my decision. I couldn't allow myself to feel feelings and continue to work here at the same time. I had to be numb because I couldn't close the shop's doors. Not yet anyway. Like my mom said, I can't close down Galaxy's without another job prospect.

"I know," I said. "But I still don't want to talk about it." Blake nodded.

"Honestly, man, this is just how I deal with death. I bet it's hard to imagine me as anything other than a social butterfly but that's not how I've always been. When someone I love dies, I tap out and lay low. I seclude myself. I escape into my own world of reading manga and watching Justice League cartoons, and I just deal with it," Blake said.

"Believe me, I get it," I said. "I miss my friends too, especially David."

Blake looked surprised – as if he wasn't expecting me to say this. I think I saw his eyes water, but I could be seeing things.

"Me too, bro. I miss all of them," Blake said. "I had so many good laughs and good times with James, Brian and Robert. They were my friends, but they felt like family. And David, I respected the hell out of him. He didn't take shit from anybody, and he always stood up for what he believed in. Foggy was a good guy with a kind heart and honest personality.'

"But you honor those that have passed on by keeping their memory alive. They'll never die as long as we're alive," Blake said.

As Blake said this, he no longer looked so sad and somber but a little chippier like his more usual self.

"You're not wrong. I'm not a religious person but that's how I see it too," I said.

"Hell yeah," Blake said with a smile. There was a short pause before he spoke again. "I'll always love Galaxy's Comics and Games, but I just don't feel safe here anymore. And like a Jordan Peele movie, I need to get the hell out, bro."

Nice. I understood that reference. I laughed.

I stepped out from behind the register. I reached out my arms. Blake gave me a big hug.

Immediately after we hugged, the door of the comic shop flew open. I heard that familiar rumbling of a chainsaw.

Rrrrrrnnn. Rrrrnnnnn. Bvvvzzzttt.

We were just a few yards away from the entrance and the killer ran towards us. Before I could even react, the chainsaw was slicing through Blake's lower back. The blood and guts splashed onto me.

"You fucking beta male," the killer said with that familiar

Ghostface voice.

I began to feel dizzy. I couldn't believe this was happening again. It's like that old saying "fool me once, shame on you. Fool me twice, shame on me." Well, I wasn't only fooled twice. If you count Foggy's murder in the parking lot, this killer is now making a third visit to the comic shop.

This time I didn't remain frozen in place. I reached over the counter and pressed the red button behind it to alert the police.

As I did this, the security guard sprung to action. He'd been standing still nearby in front of the new comic wall. He pulled out the gun from his waistband that he assured me he had a permit to carry. But before he could aim and shoot, the killer bolted forward. They swung the chainsaw like a baseball bat.

This time, the blades of the chainsaw hit the security guard's neck. Blood splattered all over the displayed comic books on the wall behind him. His head fell to the floor and rolled across it. It was still rolling when I heard the thump sound made by the rest of his body hitting the floor.

I ran toward the back door. I knew what happened to James, Brian and Robert. But the killer was blocking the way of the front door with a chainsaw. And surely if it's just a doorstop blocking the back entrance, I could body slam the back door and get through.

I had almost reached the exit when I heard those words.

"Stay the fuck there, Eric! I don't want to kill you. I just want you to listen," Anna said.

Hearing Anna's voice, I stopped dead in my tracks. With one hand on the chainsaw, Anna was holding the mask in her other. I was stunned as I looked upon her face. It was, in fact, Anna.

Anna let go of the mask and let it hang down from the

Ghostface costume. She quickly dropped the chainsaw onto the floor, pulled out a handgun and pointed it at me.

"The voice-changing device was in the mask if you were wondering," Anna said.

Perhaps I should've reacted in some way. But I couldn't. I was frozen in place. I was beyond stunned. I couldn't believe it. Anna slowly walked towards me with a gun pointed at my face.

"Oh, and that fucker's bolted shut with a chain this time. You ain't going nowhere," Anna said as she approached, referring to the back door that was a couple yards behind me. "You're staying right here and listening to what I have to say."

Chapter 17

"My father, he was a great man," Anna said. "As I've told you before, he's the one who got me into comic books. But he's in prison because of a leftist, SJW cuck like David, Foggy and Blake. A beta male writer warped his mind."

Why is Anna doing this? I didn't understand. She's not a violent person. And since when does she have a problem with so-called "SJWs"?

Not only were my friends dead, but my daily fear in owning a comic shop had come to life. Ever since ComicsGate started its online war on "SJW" comic creators, I was always looking over my shoulder. I couldn't help but suspect that some customers at my shop went home and were right-wing trolls right after buying a comic book from me.

Anna had a wild look in her eyes that I'd never seen in her before. She was usually such a laid-back person. If anything, she was the voice of reason in certain situations. That's why I confided in her after David and Foggy died. But the look in her eyes right now was something else. It was the look of repressed rage that was breaking free in a stream of consciousness.

"You see, my father read a short story anthology at the local library. He was obsessed with one particular story in the anthology. He read it over and over again. It was titled *Back on the*

Grind. I never understood his love for this story. It seemed to me like it was written by a weak-minded SJW who just complains instead of working hard. If the writer hates capitalism so much, he should just move to China or Russia for fuck's sake.'

"But I digress," Anna continued. "The story *Back on the Grind* was about a truck stop and a guy who hated working there. He hated that place so much, and so did my father after reading the story.'

"After my father searched the author's name on Facebook, he realized he really did work at a truck stop. My father sent him a private message about what a big fan he was, but the jerk didn't even reply," Anna said.

"I mean, it probably went to Message Requests, and he didn't even see it," I said.

"Whatever. That's beside the point," Anna said. "The point is this beta male's Marxist propaganda warped my father's mind. So, he did what he felt he had to do. I don't think this SJW writer even knew who my father was until the moment he killed him."

My thoughts began to race. Wait a second? Is she talking about what I think she is? I read in the news about a man who stabbed a guy and committed a mass shooting at a truck stop about 20 miles away from here. He tried to burn down the truck stop too – before local police stopped him.

"Are you talking about that nutcase who killed a bunch of people? The guy who wrote the 'Diesel Doctrine' manifesto?" I asked.

"Dad was not a nutcase! He did what he thought he had to do," Anna screamed.

She grabbed a stack of comic books off the wall and threw them at me. Reflexively, I covered my head and ducked down, but the comic books still hit me and bounced onto the floor. "The author was the 'Diesel Doctrine' guy! My father wrote a manifesto inspired by his words. I bet the author wanted those people at his workplace dead too! He just wasn't man enough to admit it.'

"My father went to prison because of Marxist propaganda – just like the comic books you sell in this store. And I'm not alone in thinking this. Not everyone is a sheep like Foggy. The ComicsGate movement is only growing as more and more comic book buyers are fed up with this shit. I hear these complaints on YouTube all the time. They made Thor a woman. They made Captain America a Black man. They made Superman gay! It's cultural Marxism," Anna said.

"Anna, there are no Marxist comic books being published by Marvel or DC. You're talking about two publishing companies that are owned by giant media corporations, Disney and Times Warner. If we have anything even close to Marxist in this store, it's probably some indie book David pre-ordered but no one else bought," I said.

"Liar!" Anna screamed, before pointing the gun up at a stack of comics on the wall and firing a single bullet.

As I was reacting to the gunshot, she lit a match and threw it onto the wall filled with new comic books. Flames began to rise. Anna pointed her gun back at me. Despite the lethal threat, my emotions were finally boiling over. I was no longer in shock. A pinch of disgust and a river of anger began flowing through my body and mind.

"I'm a liar, Anna? You're one to talk," I screamed. "You said your father was dead! You told me you read *Calvin and Hobbes* to him when he was in bed dying of brain cancer."

"He's as good as dead! He's a brainwashed cuck rotting

away in prison for the rest of his life! And the SJWs are to blame," Anna retorted.

"But what about how you read his favorite comic to him on his deathbed?" I asked.

"Well, that part I may have read someone else talking about in a blog or some shit," Anna admitted.

Chapter 18

"I am what I am and I'm not ashamed. I'm a ComicsGater. I like blood baths. And I like real men – not easily offended beta males crying about *Spider-Woman* variant covers. You, Blake and the rest of them always thought I was just sweet little Anna. But fuck that! Everyone always assumes shit. It's not right! I'm so fucking tired of it! I can't fucking stand it!" Anna yelled.

I stared at her. I didn't know what to say. I couldn't believe what I was seeing or hearing.

"Anna, you killed my friends" was all I could muster. But without skipping a beat, she continued her rant.

"You think because I'm an artsy nerd-girl with cool hair that I can't see the truth? Well, you're wrong! The cultural Marxists, the Tumblr feminists, the SJW writers – they must be stopped! They're the real sexists for thinking I can't think for myself. I'm not your shield, you cucks. Women are not a monolith!" Anna said.

The fire was spreading quickly. So far, the fire had only been contained to a few of the comic books near us. But soon enough, it will spread to the entire wall. But I was still frozen in place. Just like during Anna's first killing spree, it was as if something similar but different to a fight or flight response had kicked in. All I could do was behave like a deer caught in headlines.

"I just… I don't understand. Honestly, I suspected Adrian – you know, that former customer who got into it with David. But I never dreamed it was you who killed them. How did you fall down a ComicsGate rabbit hole? I thought you deleted your social media because of harassment…?" I asked.

"I used to make YouTube videos about how SJWs were ruining comic books. I never showed my face in these videos, but I made them. I had a few thousand people following me on Twitter because of these videos too. Some of them even bought my artwork.'

"I know it's only been about five years, but I was so young and dumb. This was in my early twenties. I was a sheltered kid, and all this culture war stuff was new to me. ComicsGate made so much sense to me back then," Anna said.

"But why?" I asked.

"I was annoyed by how Marvel and DC always tried to pander to me. It's as if they collected women and minorities like Pokémon cards. They gender bent characters to seem progressive. But it was still the same white male boomers writing these comic books," Anna said.

"That feels more like a progressive critique though. So, you're saying the capitalists who run these media companies didn't work towards any kind of meaningful representation?" I asked.

"No, Eric. I'm saying these creepy, fuck-wad comic book writers want brownie points but don't give a fuck," Anna said.

"I mean, I'm not even sure I disagree with that," I said. "But ComicsGate –"

"ComicsGate lied to me too!" Anna interrupted. "They'd tag me in their tweets. They'd bring me up as one of their female friends in their videos. It's like I wasn't a human being. I was just a name they could constantly drop when pushing their agenda. It was so fucking gross. ComicsGate turned out to be no different than the beta males using me as a shield and collecting women and minorities like Pokémon cards."

"Yeah, ComicsGate sucks," I said.

"No, humanity sucks. ComicsGate made some good points," Anna interjected.

"But when I called out ComicsGate for their hypocritical behavior, they turned their sights onto me," Anna continued. "I wasn't in line with their mob mentality. Every day I was being called names online by the very people who I thought had my back. Someone even made a video ripping up a piece of artwork they had purchased from me. After I saw that, I finally bit the bullet and did what they wanted me to do. I deleted my YouTube channel. I deactivated all my social media accounts. Aside from my Etsy shop and Etsy messages, I went off the grid."

The fire was beginning to spread to about half the store. This was becoming an extremely dangerous situation and we needed to exit the store soon. But Anna remained, standing in front of me with a gun pointed at my body.

If I were to assume Anna was telling the truth, the back door behind me would be chain locked from the outside. The only exit was the front door on the other side of the shop.

"You did what you felt you had to do," I said.

"No, I let them win. But never again! This is where you come in. This is where Galaxy's Comics & Games comes in." After she said this, it started to happen again. I felt like I was frozen in place – stunned. I stared at Anna.

"What are you talking about?" I asked.

"I didn't do this. I didn't kill those people. I didn't burn down this shop. The SJWs did. The people I killed burned it down. We can blame the SJWs. They can be like the Dark Knight to our chaotic, truth-speaking Heath Ledger," Anna said.

"What?" I proclaimed again with nothing else to say.

"Think about it, Eric. These ComicsGate idiots will eat it up. If we tell them how the SJWs burned down your comic shop, I bet we could raise a million dollars in an Indiegogo campaign. We could use the funds to self-publish a comic book – just me and you. You can write it. I can draw it. We can dedicate the Indiegogo campaign and the comic book to David, Foggy, Blake, those Yu-Gi-Oh players, the security guard and Galaxy's Comics & Games. We can dedicate it to the victims of the SJWs. It's the perfect plan."

"How?" I asked. "That's insane."

"No, my good friend. It'll be like the right-wing video game critic who was sucker punched at Gen Con. You know, the one who used the incident to raise tens of thousands of dollars in a GoFundMe campaign to pay his so-called 'medical bills.' These ComicsGate supporting suckers will give us all their hard-earned money to stick it to the libs. And you know what? I bet this Indiegogo campaign could make you more money than this busted shop that barely scrapes by," Anna said.

Ouch. That hurt. But she probably wasn't wrong on that point.

"You left a note for the police about how you were killing the 'beta males.' Why did you do that if your plan was to blame the so-called 'SJWs' for all of this?" I asked.

"Right. I'm sorry if you thought I hated you for not fitting into traditional ideas of masculinity," Anna replied. "But Dad always warned me that most men who like comic books were sissy bookworms. And those fucking assholes had it coming. They always act so virtuous but then don't even listen to me enough to realize I disagree with their white knight bullshit. They just assume I'm on their side because I'm a woman."

She didn't answer my question, but whatever. Including this statement in the note was probably a careless mistake. Either way, I still didn't understand her murderous actions. This still didn't feel like the Anna I thought I knew.

"Why are you calling people 'SJWs'? Don't you believe in social justice?" I asked.

"No, I like to think of myself as a nihilist. I certainly don't believe in fairy tales like social justice – or any of David's bullshit about how art should speak truth to power," Anna said.

"I believe that great art comes from bloodshed, plain and simple. To quote the horror comic *Random Acts of Violence*, 'art and pain are forever joined in color.' As artists, I believe we must do what we need to do to create, thrive and succeed."

"If justice existed, I wouldn't," Anna said. "You can think of me as a reckoning for every do-good motherfucker who tried to change the world faster than the world wanted to change."

As I listened to her rant, it hit me. Anna was a ComicsGater the whole time? Is it possible that she'd tormented me before and I didn't know it?

"Did you tell me to kill myself for liking *The Last Jedi*?" I asked her, knowing that I talked to her about this last week.

Anna laughed and said, "What do you think this is, Tim Burton's *Batman*? No, the Joker didn't kill Bruce Wayne's parents. And I'm sure that was just some random troll, Eric. But I'll tell you what I will do if you don't join me..."

Chapter 19

"To quote the issue of *Hack-Slash* about the guy who went on a killing spree at a comic book convention: 'I've been trying to break into this godforsaken field for 15 years… I will do things to you that would fill 1,000 of your piece-of-shit horror comics!'" Anna said.

"You know who was a huge fan of *Hack-Slash*? David. David was," I said.

"Yeah, well, David was an SJW cuck just like Tim Seeley!" Anna screamed.

"What? Then why are you quoting a comic book he wrote? I don't understand!" I screamed back at her.

"Because life is a cruel joke, that's why. The comic writers I used to love all bash my favorite YouTubers. Blake and the rest of those dead fucks acted all buddy-buddy with me. But they didn't realize I was a ComicsGater, so they talked shit to my face. And then my fellow ComicsGaters on Twitter abandoned me!'

"But I'll show them. Eric. I'll show them all. When our Indiegogo campaign is on par with all the biggest creators in ComicsGate, we'll not only be rolling in dough, but the haters will finally shut up! I'll have online support again. And I'll finally be a successful artist. Don't you want this for me? Don't you want this for us?" Anna said.

"No," I replied.

"Come on now, be reasonable. It's not like I need you alive to blame the SJWs for your comic shop burning down. I can write and draw the comic myself. I can launch the Indiegogo campaign without you. I just want you to be a part of this, Eric. You've always supported me and my artwork. I thought you of all people would understand." Anna said.

"Stop trying to gaslight me you crazy bitch!" I screamed. "Do I have to state the obvious? You're a murderer, Anna. Nothing you're talking about is anything I will ever support. Fuck your favorite YouTubers. Fuck right-wing Indiegogo projects. Fuck every single toxic fanboy and fangirl."

I made a mad dash to the front door.

Bam!

Anna shot me in my left foot, but I didn't care. I was high on adrenaline at this point. Even though Anna stood in my way, I continued my path towards the exit door.

Comics are my passion – and yet I almost stopped reading them because of poisonous fans like this. I can't believe I let them have that kind of power over me. Why should I care what these people think? These disingenuous fools aren't worth it. I can't think of a single place on earth that's worse to die than right here and now, standing next to a fucking ComicsGater.

I have news for Anna. Also, I have news for that whiny, anonymous asshole who told me to kill myself because I enjoyed *Star Wars: The Last Jedi*: I'm not dying today. And when I make it out of this fire, I'm never shutting my mouth again. Everyone will hear how much I love "woke," "SJW" comic books like *Squirrel Girl* and *Ms. Marvel*.

I smacked the gun out of Anna's hand.

"Fuck you, ComicsGate," I said.

Anna's gun landed somewhere in the fire. I had a limp, but it didn't stop me. I bolted towards the front door as fast as I could.

The fire continued to spread to all corners of the inside of the comic shop. I think every single comic book, long box and gaming table in Galaxy's Comics & Games had caught fire. By now there appeared to be more spaces covered by fire than not. However, much of the marble floor still had a path – more or less.

Anna didn't move. She stood in place behind me, appearing ready for the flames to engulf her.

"Eric, I know you pressed the red button to dial 911. But I'll die before they send me to prison like my dad," Anna said.

I was done with this. I continued towards the door of the burning comic shop without responding to her.

"Eric, my good friend, if you walk out that door, I'm staying here. Do you really want me burned alive? Do you want that on your conscience? For fuck's sake, just join me on this Indiegogo project," Anna said.

The inside of my left shoe was gushing with blood. My sock was drenched. Despite the adrenaline rush, I was starting to feel dizzy. My entire body was in agony.

Must. Make. It. To. The. Door.

I didn't want to see Anna die, but I couldn't wait around trying to save someone who didn't want to be saved. Hopefully when the firefighters and paramedics arrive, they'll rescue her from this burning building.

Despite the adrenaline, I was starting to slow down on my walk to the door. It probably had something to do with the fire on my clothing and the bullet in my foot.

"I'm not committing suicide by cop. I'm a white woman.

That's too risky. If I'm dying, it'll be here in these flames," Anna yelled across the room.

I think it wasn't just my clothing, but parts of my skin were burning too. I didn't care. I had finally made it to the front door. I reached my hand out and I opened it.

"Well, fuck you too, Social Justice Warrior!" Anna screamed at me.

I stumbled out of the comic shop and collapsed onto the ground. The adrenaline rush was starting to die down.

I rolled across the sidewalk, putting out the fire on my clothing and bringing myself further and further away from the burning building. Even though I was no longer burning, every part of my body that contacted the concrete was putting me in even more tremendous pain.

But I didn't care. I made it. I will survive.

Chapter 20

Two months later…

"Well, Eric, there are a lot of impressive applicants, but we'll let you know in a week. We are looking for younger journalists with fresh perspectives, and I believe you fit the bill." I was inside one of the offices for a local newspaper. The job interview was wrapping up. I think I was nailing it.

A lot has changed in the last couple of months. Galaxy's Comics & Games is no more. It was burned to a crisp. I received a handsome financial reimbursement after filing an insurance claim. However, there's no way the check I received fully covered the actual cost of some of the rare and valuable comic books and Magic: The Gathering cards that were lost in the fire. But as a certain self-proclaimed nihilist used to say, "it is what it is."

Normies, man – they just don't get it. This is why so-called "collector's insurance" exists in addition to store and homeowners' insurance.

Anna didn't make it out of the flames alive. By the time the firefighters and paramedics arrived, it was too late. The paramedics carried me away on a stretcher and treated my injuries. But like my comic shop, Anna had become nothing more or less than a memory. After the news broke of her crimes, all the art-work in her Etsy store sold out almost immediately. I guess some people are really drawn to a tortured artist with a violent life story. I've been told Anna's cousin and roommate Holly handled the shipments and donated the profit to charity.

I have several scars on my body now. There's a very notice-able gash and a red bubble on my face. Fortunately, my visible scars aren't too gruesome looking. But for the rest of my life, I'll have to tell some version of the story of my escape from a burning building.

For the past few weeks, I've been working second shift at a popular, 24-hour convenience store chain. It wasn't hard getting the job with my years of customer service experience. But I've kept my eye on the prize – using my bachelor's degree for a journalism or computer science job. I've continued to apply for professional jobs non-stop.

"Thanks," I said. "If you do hire me, you won't regret it." I shook the interviewer's hand, said goodbye, and walked out the office and towards the building's elevator to go home.

That song by the Interrupters was stuck in my head again – the one about a match and kerosene.

I don't have to own a comic shop to promote comics. After all, David never owned a comic shop but his passion for the me-dium was infectious. I can do that too. Maybe that's one way I can honor David's memory. I can honor Blake's memory by trying to be more outgoing and easier to get along with. As for Foggy, I feel like I've already honored his memory. After all, our last conversation was about how he wanted the killer brought to justice.

When looking back at the massacres at the comic shop, it feels like a bad dream. It's a chaotic blur with missing pieces that I can't remember. Although I occasionally do remember these moments when they come flashing back to me, sometimes at the most inopportune times.

I still can't believe who it turned out was committing these massacres. Maybe I could've caught the warning signs and cries for help early on. Maybe I could've stopped Anna from going down the poisonous, online rabbit hole that she did. Despite everything she did, I can't shake the feeling that I failed her as a friend.

Not everything is what it seems. Thinking about the identity of the ComicsGate killer, I realize that I shouldn't have ever been so quick to fear strangers. Sometimes an abuser, a tormentor or the villain of the story is right there in front of your face the whole time – and it's not who you assume based on your implicit biases and preconceived notions.

I'm not a nihilist and I never will be. However, sometimes it feels like nothing makes sense and nothing matters. We see horrible acts committed in our name, and we feel powerless to stop them. It can feel like the world is on a path to self-destruction, but no one listens to those of us trying to divert it. We feel like there's nothing we can do but accept our doom. And yet, somehow, some way, we still stand tall, ready to fight for our ideas. A lot of us nerdy and/or creative types have had these feelings before. We've felt like the sole survivor at the end of a horror story – lonely and distraught but unyielding.

Was Blake's death my fault? I had already blamed myself for what happened to David, Foggy and Blake's Yu-Gi-Oh playing buddies, Brian, Robert and James. But that was only two incidents – with only one of them actually happening inside the walls of Galaxy's. Blake's death is something I didn't prevent like the mayor from the movie *Jaws*. Mayor Larry Vaughn continued to keep the beaches open even when he knew a killer shark was lurking in the waters. He did it because the town was dependent on tourist dollars. The town's economy needed the money from those vacationing, swimming and basking in the summertime sun. In a similar vein, I didn't close the comic shop when I knew the masked killer had never been caught. I reopened not once but twice before losing Blake.

But then again, there's more to it than that, isn't there? Galaxy's wasn't a vacation spot like Amity Island. It was more than just a place of business. Galaxy's was a community. Granted, like my father said, the shop was my only source of income, and I didn't want my livelihood disrupted. However, this wasn't the only reason why I reopened the shop after the murders. I wasn't behaving purely out of greed. I was trying desperately to hold onto a semblance of hope. Galaxy's Comics & Games was something I didn't want me or anyone else to have to lose.

David once told me that he often worried about people thinking he was weird, annoying or a burden. However, when he was inside the comic shop or around the comic convention crowd, he said he no longer had these anxieties. In fact, he said we're some of the only people who he never had to worry about this around.

Maybe I could've waited until the ComicsGate killer had been caught by the police before reopening the store. Perhaps it was against my better judgment to keep the doors open. But how long would the shop have had to stay closed? Anna would've likely waited until I reopened the store before she killed again, especially considering her ultimate plan. The police were chasing leads like "what enemies do David and Foggy have outside of the shop?" and "does 'beta male' mean something other than what the comic shop owner told us?" If I'd closed down the store, it's possible they never would've apprehended or even suspected the actual perpetrator.

With slim profit margins, if I'd closed the shop for just a month or two, that could've spelled an end to Galaxy's. What would I have done with the new comic books during that time? I wouldn't be selling several months' worth of new comics, so I'd likely have to stop ordering them. It isn't like the publishers would stop publishing new comics or Diamond and Lunar would stop distributing them. They'd continue to release them while I was temporarily not buying and stocking them. Customers at Galaxy's would have to find another shop to fill the gap in their comic book subscriptions. During the closure, some of the regular gaming customers might end up finding another shop to play their games too.

In other words, it's possible the killings never would've ended without either Galaxy's Comics & Games permanently closing or a final confrontation. It seems like it was one or the other – and no third option. Sure, Galaxy's has become history, anyway. But hindsight is twenty-twenty. I think I did the best I could with what I knew. That's all anyone can do in life. Sure, most of us haven't dealt with a chainsaw-wielding psychopath dressed up like the killer from a popular horror movie. But you can't say your life isn't absurd sometimes too.

After the elevator reached the first floor, I walked out of the office building. I was feeling pretty good about myself and hopeful for the future. This new career path looked bright.

As I walked out of the front door, I saw him standing a few yards away from the entrance. It was Adrian. He was wearing a sleek, black trench coat and black combat boots with white laces. He had ripped black jeans and a black T-shirt with the Yellow Lantern Corps symbol.

The expression on Adrian's face was twisted into one of rage. He was gripping a large hunting knife. His bared fist wasn't raised up but was hanging in the direction of the ground. The blade was facing behind him.

"I heard you've been talking shit about me, bro," he said.

NERD CON
KPW WAS HERE!
AMERICAN BUG
RINE

ACKNOWLEDGEMENTS

If you self-publish a book, like it or not, you've joined an ideological war on the establishment. You're among a ragtag group of rebels facing off against a powerful empire. Because the more successful your book is, the more you're showing these companies that, like a straight shaving razor, the old ways are unnecessary. We don't have to "get published" to have a book. To quote a poem I wrote in *American Bug*, "we can make great art ourselves without kissing corporate ass."

Those of us in self-publishing can sometimes think of ourselves as lone wolves. It's you against the world. You have no one you can count on except yourself. While there's some truth to this way of thinking, it's not the whole picture. It's true that I did this book my way. I brought this book to life without a shred of approval from gatekeepers in the publishing industry.

Here's the problem with this way of thinking, though. No one accomplishes anything alone. Nowhere in the multiverse could *Massacre at the Comic Shop* exist without the contributions of others. And everyone who helped bring this book to life deserves all the thanks in the world.

First, I'd like to thank everyone who backed *Massacre at the Comic Shop* on Kickstarter:

A. Smith	Jorge Santiago Jr.
Alex Stritar	Joseph W. Duis
Andy P.	Justin Anderson
Ann LaCorte	K. "Cyanide" Stauffer
Ashley Danley	Kristen Dahm
Barbara Ann Siemens	Lalinda De La Fuente
Ben Lacy	Louis Wire
Bradley J. Smith	Marimonica
Brandon Angelo Moncada	Michael Whalen
Brandon Bloxdorf	Mika Exley
- Apollo City Comics	Nico Martinez
Cassey Eisch	Nicole D'Andria
Catherine & Sarah Satrum	Onrie Kompan
Claire	Pagan Hayes
Dennis Ulanowski	Phil Falco
Dierdre Roberts	Phillip J. Thomas
Donna Ulanowski	Pistol Pete
Dren Productions	Richard Novak
Ed "Number One 'Drive My	Robert J. Sodaro
Car' Fan" Kolkebeck	Ryan F. Skelly
Elliott Mondry	Ryan Francis
Eric Palicki	sKooTeR millS
Felix Medina	Sophie Majewski
The Ghost of Adam Smith	Steve Aultz
Grant Williams	Sydney Baker
Howie Silver	That Collage Girl
Jamie Badtke-Matter	Timothy P. Rossi
Jess Wood	Tom Kelly

There are so many people who I talked to online, at Chicago area comic shops and at conventions who inspired a sentence or a paragraph in this book. If I tried to list every single one of you, the Acknowledgments would be way too long. Also, if I'm being perfectly honest, I'd still probably forget someone, anyway. So, for the sake of concision, I'd like to thank **the comic book community** for the inspiration you provided. Without my many conversations with comic book readers, collectors and creators, this book would not exist. Even if I don't mention you by name, you know who you are.

More specifically, thanks so much to **Kevin P. West**. You illustrated the poem "MAGA Hat" in my book of poetry, *American Bug*, with a breathtaking illustration. And you did it again with *Massacre at the Comic Shop*'s front and back cover illustrations. You went above and beyond my expectations and brought to life the massacre at Galaxy's Comics & Games. Your drawing of the rusty, bloody chainsaw even caused me to go back and add a few details to the book's manuscript. I'm so happy to know a fellow horror fan like you who really "gets it." Your bone chilling artwork successfully captured the essence of this book and for that, I am eternally grateful.

Next, I'd like to thank **Audrey Clément** for designing the *Massacre at the Comic Shop* logo as well as the book's front and back covers. The back cover design is beautiful, and the logo is nothing short of perfect. I love how you managed to cover up as little as possible of the front cover artwork. For instance, even if the Nerd Con sign on the front cover was partially covered up, the reader can still see it in all its glory on the back cover. I was really worried that after the cover's text was added, something in the artwork was going to be lost. But somehow, you made it work out, so this didn't happen. For that, I really appreciate you and all your hard work.

Thanks to **Deirdre Roberts** who was the official editor on the book and has been a longtime supporter of my writing. Her proofreading was essential to the final product. There was a repeated misspelling that I'm so glad you caught. It's too embarrassing to admit what it was in writing. Let's just say it was something a comic book nerd such as myself really shouldn't have misspelled. Deirdre also wrote the Foreword to *American Bug* and has backed every one of my Kickstarters. Thanks to **Destinee Jones** as well. She read an early draft of *Massacre at the Comic Shop* and gave me essential critiques that caused me to change certain characterizations. This book wouldn't be as good without you. Thanks as well to **Mika Exel**. Unlike some of the others I'm thanking here, I never sent her the entire manuscript of this story. However, very early on in the writing process, she read an early draft of a few of the chapters. Your moral support and proofreading are very much appreciated. And I wish you all the luck in the world in your future writing endeavors.

When writing the book's Foreword, **Tim Seeley** fucking killed it. The first time I read it, I felt like standing up and cheering. Thank you, Tim, for "getting it" and understanding what I was trying to do. It's an honor to be able to have your name attached to this book. Thanks as well to my fellow Chicago Writers Association member **Jennifer Worrell**. She read an early draft of *Massacre at the Comic Shop* and gave me her thoughts and opinions. To be quite frank, your reassurance that my story could resonate with a non-comic book fan meant a lot to me. And I'm honored to be able to use your review quote on the back cover of this book. Thanks as well to my stepfather **Grant Williams** for your extremely generous Kickstarter pledge and for your many years of moral support for my writing. Even if there are plenty of other Kickstarter backers who helped make this book happen, you're still what I'd call the Executive Producer of this project.

Thank you, **Phil Falco**, for giving me both inspiration and moral support. Not long before I began writing *Massacre at the Comic Shop*, I read a horror comic that Phil wrote called *Haunting*. It's a very character-based story with the themes of grief, trauma and failed relationships. Phil's horror story inspired me to finally write a horror story of my own. Also, talking to Phil at a convention helped cement some of the core ideas I had for *Massacre at the Comic Shop* – most notably, who the killer was going to be. Similarly, I have to thank Tim Seeley again and **Eric Palicki**. Conversions with them at the same convention also helped me figure out the direction to take in my horror story.

It may seem trivial. However, I can't forget to thank my friends **Ed Kolkebeck**, **Alex Stritar**, **Ryan Skelly**, **Tim Rossi**, **Peter Morrison** and **Londyll Dabs** for their moral support for this story and this book. While I've been reading newspaper comic strips since my childhood, Ed was kind of the guy who first got me into comic books back in the day. He was also the first person to read an early draft of *Massacre at the Comic Shop* in its entirety. Ed's thought-provoking advice was instrumental. Alex, who owns Zone Comics & Games in Homewood, IL, also gave me fantastic advice. I don't remember who it was exactly who came up with the name "Galaxy's Comics & Games," but I know that I decided on that name during a conversation with him.

Conversations with **That Collage Girl** (as she wants to be referred to here) helped me craft some of the most important dialogue in the story. Let's just say that the killer's monologue in the story's climax wouldn't be the same without her help. So, thank you for that. In the same vein, I can't forget to thank **Barbara Ann Siemens** for helping make the *Buffy the Vampire Slayer*-related dialogue better. Conversations with you about *Buffy* helped improve some of my favorite dialogue in *Massacre at the Comic Shop*.

I'd also like to thank **anyone who helped promote *Massacre at the Comic Shop*** – whether it was sharing the Kickstarter link on social media, plugging it in your own Kickstarter update or telling your friends and family about my book. More specifically, thanks to **the Apollo City Comics podcast** who had me on as a guest. It was fucking amazing being able to chat with you guys for an hour about my Kickstarter for this book, comic book fandom and the horror genre. Also, thanks to **the Drunken Pen Writing podcast** for having me on the show as well. I got to promote the *Massacre at the Comic Shop* Kickstarter, plug my other books and chat with you guys about the publishing industry and the writing process. I had a blast on both of these podcast shows. And I appreciate the exposure.

Finally, I'd like to wholeheartedly thank **Jorge Santiago Jr**. While he had no direct involvement in my latest endeavor, *Massacre at the Comic Shop*, he's still been my right-hand man in self-publishing. He designed the Starving Author Press logo, designed all three of my previous books and drew the front and back cover artwork for *American Bug* and *As the Moonlight Shines*. Simply calling Jorge a "cover artist" or a "graphic designer" would be understating the role he's played in my books. Like I said, "right-hand man" is a more accurate descriptor. Jorge helped me through much of the self-publishing process with an enormous amount of patience. While he was too busy for direct involvement this time around, Jorge backed *Massacre at the Comic Shop* on Kickstarter and he signed a handful of copies of *American Bug* that were mailed out to higher level Kickstarter backers. Thank you so much for everything. My journey as a small print publisher wouldn't be the same without you.

ABOUT THE AUTHOR

Nick Ulanowski is a journalist, a poet, a novelist and the owner of Starving Author Press. *Massacre at the Comic Shop* is his fourth book, but it won't be his last. His previous works include *As the Moonlight Shines*, *American Bug* and *Diesel Doctrine and the Temporarily Embarrassed Millionaires*. Nick strongly believes in the power of words and hopes that his will continue to speak truth to power.